THE VAMPIRE TRIALS

THE SUMMONING

STORM SONG

Dedicated to my sister Jade.

Thanks for telling Grandma I write Vampire Porn

CHAPTER 1

A gust of brisk midnight breeze brushed over my collarbones and sent a shiver down my spine. I shuddered as I forced the crooked zipper of my winter jacket all the way up and shoved my hands in my pockets. The spring that year had brought in a cold front unlike any we had seen in decades.

My heart thudded so loud in my chest that I could hardly hear the faint hum of the famous New York City traffic. I curled my sweaty hands into fists and shoved them into my pockets. Most humans didn't dare go out after nightfall, not in a hundred years. Ever since the Great Takeover, they knew what kind of fates awaited them in the dark; we all knew.

But unfortunately, life didn't stop after nightfall, and neither did my mother's need for medicine. She had run out of her meds for one of her complicated medical conditions days ago, and she couldn't handle it anymore. The effects of not having them were horrible. I couldn't stand to watch her suffer like that any longer, which was what brought me to Doc's Pharmacy at midnight.

"Doc? You there?" I half whispered tapping my fists lightly against the metal door of the pharmacy. I glanced over my shoulder nervously. Even speaking outside at night was dangerous. Everyone knew the vampires had supersonic hearing; it was what made them good predators.

And our inability to listen to the city curfew was what made us good prey.

There was a rustling behind the door. It cracked open just a bit, and Doc peeked his head out. He offered a warm and silent smile before pulling his head back inside and sticking his arm through. He clutched the white paper bag in his hand, and I graciously pulled it from him without uttering a single thank you. The door carefully closed, and I heard the twelve locks he had slide into their places.

It hurt not being able to say thank you, or to ask him how his wife was doing, but that came with the territory. The pharmacy usually wasn't even open this late, but he was a friend of the family and agreed. He said he was already going to be awake because of the broadcast of the summoning anyway, and he knew that my mom was having a hard time.

I pulled the paper bag close and flinched at the sound of it rustling. Any sound was too much sound.

As quickly as I had come, I turned around and made my way back up the vacant street. The dim, yellow light from the streetlamps was the only thing that lit the way, and the stars were my only companion.

The city at night was a completely different world. Even the beat up sidewalks and old apartment buildings seemed to twist and turn differently in the faded light.

I held my breath as I walked. I hoped that there wasn't anyone else with the same idea as me. I prayed I wouldn't pass another terrified human trying to sneak in an errand. I couldn't risk someone else blowing my cover- not tonight.

Maybe all the vamps are busy; it's a big night for their kind. I thought. I almost scared myself with how spitefully I lingered on the words. My mother had always raised me to be compassionate and kind. Even now, she always preached that we shouldn't hate the vampires just because they basically ruled the city. But as hard as I tried, I couldn't do it. I couldn't give them a pass. I probably got it from my father's side. I couldn't keep him out of my mind. Every second of every day, there was a piece of him with me; unfortunately, it was usually his anger. I was sweet like my mom, but I had an angry streak like my dad. I was a walking contradiction, and it had definitely spoiled its share of opportunities for me. Relationships were almost impossible because I could never find someone that could handle both.

There was a loud noise behind me as a trashcan clashed loudly against the cement, pulling me from my thoughts. I flinched, mentally kicking myself for how long I had let myself go on autopilot. I knew better than that, but unfortunately, getting lost in my thoughts was another thing I had gotten from *dear old dad* after he had passed away.

I hope to god that it was just another fucking stray.

I told myself that it was and picked up my pace, but my heart wasn't so easily convinced. I could barely function with it beating so thunderously inside of my chest.

Behind me, there was another crash, closer now as another metal can bit the dust.

Stupid kids. It's probably some immature teenagers trying to get themselves killed.

I thought it, but that time, I didn't even believe it. In this age, even immature teenagers knew better than to be out after dark. Sure, there was still some danger during the day with the few vamps that had day powers, but most came out at night. And the majority of them didn't give a fuck about humans.

I picked up the pace and tried my hardest not to think about every horrific death story I had heard on the news. I focused on putting one foot in front of the other and clutched the medicine tightly.

Mom needs this, and she's going to get it. There isn't a thing in the world that's going to stop me, I pep talked myself as I turned another corner.

A window shattered behind me, and I yelped. I knew I shouldn't have, and that it was basically signing my own death certificate.

I even threw my hands up to my lips as it was coming out to try to catch it, but it was no use. It came out, and I knew that was the beginning of the end.

A loud hoop filled the air, followed by a series of hair-raising cackles. If I didn't know better, I would have thought I was being chased by a hoard of circus clowns.

But I did know better, and the only clown on the streets that night was me.

I instantly threw my pace into overdrive and broke out into an all-out run. I didn't care how stupid I looked trying to run with my heavy coat, clutching the paper pharmacy bag. I had to make it home. My mother needed her medicine.

"Look boys, we got ourselves a runner!" a man cackled hysterically. He was laughing so hard that he was almost intelligible.

I knew in an instant who was trailing me…members of Invicta. I knew I was in deep shit. Invicta was a notorious, magical, drug smuggling vampire gang that nearly ran the city right alongside the governors. Aside from their violence and killings, they also were the largest sellers of *ice*. Ice was a mystical drug that was passed around the supernatural community. Not only did it make them insanely strong and incredibly fast, its high made them cackle like hyenas.

And from the sounds of it, this guy was as high as a kite. A series of cackles joined in on the non-existent joke.

I listened as close as I could just like my dad taught me and tried to decipher how many there were by the location of the echoes and the pitch.

There's got to be six- wait no, seven.

This was new territory for me. When my dad was alive, I had no reason to go on these escapades. No reason to be out late at night by myself, but over the last few years since he'd died, it seemed like I'd found myself in these situations more and more often. First, it was the vampire in the supermarket with day powers trying to attack me in the bread aisle. Then it was the alleyway vamp that pounced on me at sunset. I didn't even want to think about the vampire perv who'd been tapping on my window trying to oblige me to open my window and invite him in.

What the hell is with the sudden interest in little ol' me? I thought as I gasped for air and took a sharp left. My apartment building came into view at the end of the street, and a wave of relief swept over me. I was almost there, only feet away from safety. As quickly as a sliver of hope was given to me, it was all taken when my foot snagged a piece of lifted concrete in the sidewalk that hadn't been fixed, and I was sent spiraling to the ground. The paper bag flew from my hands up into the air, and before it could hit the ground, a bony man with a dirty blonde mullet dashed to it with vamp speed and caught it midair. He wore a jean jacket with the sleeves ripped off for a makeshift vest and black leather pants.

Invicta.

I scrambled to flip over on my back and realized that I was surrounded by a circle of five guys that looked almost identical. They each had wide, crooked smiles plastered across their stained red lips. By the look of it, I would have gladly guessed that I wasn't the only person they'd caught with their guard down that night.

I didn't say a word. I didn't beg for mercy or try to explain myself because I knew that was what they wanted. They didn't just want to feed off of my blood, they wanted to feed off of the high of having power over me. The high of being the ones in charge of whether I lived or died. I refused to give them any more satisfaction than them seeing me already on the ground. I held my tongue and looked up at them with a fire in my eyes. I was sure all the words that I didn't say came spewing out at them in the form of the nastiest look I'd ever had the pleasure of giving someone. They knew in my mind, I was screaming *fuck you* at the top of my lungs. But even if they weren't hopped up on ice, they wouldn't have cared.

My eyes flitted over to the one that clutched my mother's meds in his hands. He didn't know it, but he held her life in his hands too. I didn't dare let him catch on, or god knows he would have chucked the bag all the way to central park, and I would have never seen it again.

"Well boys, it looks like we found ourselves a midnight snack," he said. His drawl was southern and made me question what he was even doing on the outskirts of New York City anyway.

He smirked. "And lucky for us, this one actually looks like one too."

My stomach churned, and I spit at the ground in disgust which made him let out a howl like I'd just told him the funniest joke he'd ever heard. He threw his head back and let his voice be carried off by the wind and drowned out by the distant sounds of traffic. He didn't care who heard; the only people out in traffic at this time were supernaturals who didn't have to worry about being on the bottom of the food chain anyway.

"Wait a minute, boss," a wiry kid said from the circle. "Isn't that her?"

The man turned and squinted his eyes at me before a look of recognition swept across his face.

"Well, I'll be. It is her. You, little lady, have a lot of dangerous people looking for you." He smirked. "Which just means more fun for me." His devilish grin revealed his pearly white fangs hiding behind his upper lip.

I looked at him, confused. I wanted to ask him what the hell that meant, and why it was so important. It couldn't hurt. I'd probably be dead soon, but I was immediately cut off by a high-pitched hissing sound that came from above us. I looked just in time to see a smoke bomb being launched from one of the windows of my apartment building that towered next to us. As quickly as the first came, a second came from a window down the hall, and even a third sailed out from the top floor. All three sailed to the ground with a thick tail of smoke trailing closely behind. The dark green gas quickly seeped out and engulfed the gang, sending them into a fit of combined cackling and coughing. They all dropped to their knees, including the boss man that was holding my mother's medication hostage.

I saw my opportunity to bolt, and I took it. I jumped to my feet and dashed to the paper bag, swiping it before the Invicta members even knew what was going on. As they all choked and gasped

12

around me, I thanked my lucky stars that the tarragon bombs were only toxic to vampires. It looked like it hurt…a lot.

With the pharmacy bag in hand, I made my break and slid into the door to my building. I quickly bolted up the stairs to make it to the third floor. I passed Mrs. Camino on the first floor with her door wide open.

"Thank you so much, Mrs. Camino," I panted as I passed her door.

"It's no problem, mija," she replied, still sitting at her window and watching the vamps writhe from the pain of her smoke bomb. The sixty-year-old still found just as much pleasure fighting back then as she did decades ago in her time in the resistance. I wasn't surprised she had come to my aid, but I was grateful, and that was all that mattered.

I pushed past her door and made my way up to the third floor before slipping into our apartment. I slid all of the deadbolts into their place and finally let myself feel relieved.

"Mom, what did I tell you about being that close to the window?" I muttered. I tried to act upset, but I was actually impressed that she'd gotten into her wheelchair and had placed herself in front of the window to gaze. I was even more impressed that the smoke bomb she had tossed actually made its way to us down there.

I peered down out the window. Below in the streets, the vamps were still recovering.

"Those things were potent. How much tarragon was in them?"

"A hell of a lot by the looks of them," she wheezed but smiled.

Her tired eyes said it all, so I let it be.

"Well I got your meds. I got here in one piece, and the summoning hasn't started yet. So I have those going for me," I smiled. My response seemed to comfort her as I saw her loosen her tight grip on the arm rests.

"Let the summoning begin," she smiled at her own twisted joke.

CHAPTER 2

I tossed my mother her pills and grabbed a bag of chips as she switched on the small television that was perched in our broom closet of a living room. It wasn't much, but in New York City, for two humans, it was a hell of a lot, and it was what I gladly called home. There wasn't any other place that I would have rather been.

"Honey?" My mother looked up at me, and her tired eyes met mine. "Can you move Dad out of the way so we can see the whole screen?" She gestured toward the simple silver urn that sat proudly on the TV stand.

I nodded and carefully slid it aside more before taking my seat again. I glanced over at my mother. She was clearly already feeling a lot better with the help of the medicine, but even a blind man could see that her disease was getting worse. Her cancer was spreading, and there wasn't a damn thing that I could do about it, and that was what tore me up the most. The vampires, I could fight for her. The looters and rioters, I would take on without a second glance. But how do you kick stage four cancer's ass?

The television automatically clicked on, and the government sanctioned station took over. There was no use trying to change it because for the next 24 hours, the broadcast that was happening live would play on a loop until all of the summoned reported in for their intake. It was required that every non-supernatural citizen watch the broadcast. Every human in New York's sleep schedule was fucked anyway, so most of us tuned in without a bother, even though it was on in the wee hours of the morning. Being a human, you learned to adapt fast to whatever kept you alive. Sometimes that meant going for a grocery run at noon, and sometimes, it meant staying awake all night like the supernaturals did. We did whatever worked best for us.

Behind me, there was a rapping on the dining room window. I turned to see the Invicta mob boss tapping his fingernail lightly on the window. His ugly smile still clung to his face, but his eyes and nose were red, and he had a gash in this cheek from clawing at his face, trying to force his lungs to work again.

"Just leave it, Scarlett. It's not worth the time."

I shrugged and got up from the couch and made my way to the window. All I was missing was the long and outdrawn speech. It was the same every five years anyway from what I'd heard. I made my way to the window and tapped my fingernail against the glass too, just to piss him off.

He looked at me seriously and cocked his head to one side. "You want to open the window and invite me in."

I let my eyes space out and focused on the faded city lights out in the distance. "I want to open the window and let you in," I said in a monotone voice as I made my way to the window and wrapped my fingers around the handle. "Not!" I laughed in his face. "You and I both know that you can't oblige me while I'm in a house that you haven't been invited into. No invite means no brainwashing; better luck next time, bud." I let out a genuine laugh and relished in the look of pure fury in his blazing eyes. He pounded his fists against the window, but the glass held up. I breathed a sigh of relief that my father had us install the shatterproof windows throughout the entire apartment. It really was an investment that paid off in the end. I silently admired his dedication to ripping me limb from limb. I couldn't think of anything I wanted enough to free climb a five-story building to get.

I grabbed a drink and found my place back in the worn-down leather couch that we had inherited from the previous renters. "Did I miss anything important?"

"I don't know." Her lips pursed together tightly. "They just announced that in a few moments, they are going to share with us some new rules about the Vampire Trials, and who it's going to affect."

I didn't think much of it. At twenty, I had only ever lived through a history of 3 matches. There was still a lot about the customs and why the hell it actually took place to learn for me.

I pulled my snow white hair out of my face and into a low ponytail before tossing another chip inside of my mouth. My stomach churned as I watched the live broadcast. It was the first one that we'd ever had to watch without my father, and that stung more than anything. He hated the trials. He despised them with a passion, but why wouldn't he? As the leader of the biggest underground human resistance organization, the trials went against everything he believed in.

Since the beginning of the Great Takeover when supernaturals came out of hiding and overthrew the humans, the city of New York had been divided into three different triads. Each triad was ruled by a glorified vampire overlord called a governor who basically got to do whatever he wanted. With the rise of vampires to power, things got crazy with vampires killing whoever they wanted whenever they pleased, and the human population dropped drastically, which wasn't too good for the vampires who needed human blood to survive. As a counter measure, the governors introduced laws on when and how vampires were allowed to feed, but when that wasn't enough to keep both populations at bay, the trials were what they came up with. It's a sick and twisted way to get humans to kill each other, pit the different triads against each other, and let the vampires get a little power trip in the process.

Each year, three candidates from each triad are chosen, and they have 24 hours to tell everyone they've ever loved goodbye and head to Trials Manor to prepare to die. Only one person comes out alive, and their triad is the one that will be spared from the free for all slaughter that makes it legal to kill any adult male for a twenty-four hour period. The other two triads are out of luck.

When I was younger, I didn't fully understand it. It was something that had happened for my whole life, so I didn't know the difference. It sounded like a horror story, something out of a late night movie, but now it made me feel like I wanted to puke every time it came to mind. It was barbaric; it was sadistic, and it was sadly, one hundred percent real.

The commencement ceremony finished, and the three vampire governors walked onto the screen. They each wore fancy black suits, designer no doubt, with matching ties. Even through the television screen they reeked of wealth and privilege. They stood tall with their heads held high, enjoying every minute of their power, no doubt.

But I had a feeling that everything wasn't perfect in their lives. Over the last few years, there had been reports of more and more vampire retaliations. The vamps didn't like the rules, and with the introduction of the magical drugs into their systems, they were finally bold enough to say it. Every day there were more and more stories of vamps breaking the *no killing in daylight* rules, luring people into dark alleyways and vampire clubs away from the stinging touch of the sunlight, only to rip them apart.

I smiled smugly, enjoying imagining how horrible they must feel watching their twisted empire crumbling piece by piece. I knew if my father hadn't been killed in the last purge five years ago, he would have been smiling too.

"Welcome everyone, to the twentieth annual summoning ceremony," the governor of my triad, triad three, took the podium. "Twenty is a big number, one that our ancestors only dreamed of seeing. But here we are, one hundred years later."

The crowd of rich vampire socialites cheered and whooped, but I knew that there wasn't a single human watching whose lunch didn't threaten to come up just at the sound.

"We have heard the cries of our people. We know you're discontent. There isn't enough blood to go around in the blood banks, and there aren't enough donors to keep up with high demand," the governor sighed.

"Donors? You mean human blood bags that you oblige to dedicate their lives to being drained," I seethed, talking to the television.

My mother turned to me and sighed, "Scarlett, you sound like your father."

I groaned. My mother was the kind of woman who was sweet-too sweet. She was a 'what happens is meant to happen' kind of woman. She always had been, but it was kicked into overdrive with her cancer diagnosis. She always hated when my father tried to buck the system, it made her uncomfortable. But at some point in time, she must have agreed with him, otherwise I never would have been born. I wondered where that version of my mother lay, somewhere deep inside, sheltered inside a cocoon of this version's worry and fear.

"This is why we've decided to make some changes to mark our hundred-year reign. These changes will take place immediately, and I believe that they are important to both the supernatural and human populations in order to keep the peace between all. In the beginning, these changes will be hard to adjust to. They'll be different, but we believe that the harmony is worth the discomfort in the long run."

The two governors that stood behind him nodded, and the crowd went wild before they even knew what the stupid changes were.

Sheep, I snorted in my mind.

"That's why, starting today, we are making an amendment to our traditional rules. As of this moment, men are not the only ones who will be summoned to partake in the trials. The names of every able-bodied woman over the age of 18 from each triad have now been added to the summoning pot."

My heart sank into my shoes.

"What? No. They can't do that. Can they mom?" My head whipped in her direction, and a wave of panic swept over me.

"In the days of equality, yes, they can, sweetie."

"No. That's bullshit!" I jumped to my feet. Her composure was only making the decision burn worse.

"Language, Scarlett."

I balled my hands into fists and huffed.

"And respectively, during the purge, women are now added to the penalty free list as well."

My mother and I turned to look at each other. Now the look of worry and horror spread to her face too. "All men and women over the age of 18 will be penalty free."

"Killable, he means. All adults. What the hell!" The room spun and I felt sick. It couldn't get worse. None of it could possibly get worse.

I lowered myself into the couch and phased out the rest of the opening speech. I didn't need to hear the details. The details didn't matter. All I cared about were the thousands of people who were going to be dead soon. All the orphaned children who would grow up in the broken system, only to be forced to relive the same trauma every five years. It was insane.

"Scarlett," my mother pulled me from my thoughts. "They're starting with triad three this time."

"What?" I turned to the TV in confusion. "They start with one. They always start with one! What the hell are they doing?"

I watched as the assistants carted the large, metal spinner onto the stage and used the crank to spin it, sifting all of the slips with names on them together.

The governor pulled a slip of paper from the container, and a fake smile graced his lips. "And what do you know, we have our first female contender. Scarlett Johnson from triad three, you have been summoned."

CHAPTER 3

I didn't hear a word the governor said after he announced that I'd been summoned. I just sat in front of the television with my mouth hanging open. There were so many thoughts racing through my mind that all I heard inside my head was a low hum of white noise. Beside me, I saw my mother sobbing into her hands. Her body shook violently with each large gasp. If I were in my right mind, I would have comforted her, pat her on the back, or something. But I was in shock, and my mind refused to communicate with my body.

Scarlett Johnson from triad three, you have been summoned.

The words echoed around inside my head like a ping pong ball. Nine little words. They were barely enough to form a sentence, but together, they still managed to completely annihilate life as I knew it.

Emotions flowed through me in waves. First was the shock, then the disbelief came through me like a freight train. It was a joke. It had to be. Or nightmare, one of the ones that feels so real that you cry tears of joy that it's not when you wake up.

Then the fear took over and squeezed my chest like an angry python. I felt like I couldn't breathe. The walls and the ceilings were closing in on me, threating to pin me down with their weight. Last came the sadness. It came when I glanced over at my mother. She had finally stopped sobbing, and all that was left of her was a hollow, sad shell. Besides her sister that lived across town, I was all she had left. A dead husband, and a soon to be dead, only daughter. That was the legacy that she would have to live out the last few days of her life with. I looked at her, and my heart ached. She was my best and only friend. I'd spent the last five years caring for her, and we'd gotten closer than I had ever imagined. They took her husband, and now, the vamps were going to take her daughter too.

I wasn't going to let that happen. I jumped to my feet in an instant and sprinted to my bedroom. It wasn't a far jog in the shoebox of an apartment, and for once, I saw that as an advantage. I ripped the doors of my closet open so fast that I thought they were going to rip off and pulled down my beat up duffel bag from the top shelf. It was weathered, and the pink fabric was peeling, but I didn't care. It was all I had, and all I had was good enough. From the closet, I hurried to the dresser and pulled out my clothes in handfuls. I didn't care what I grabbed or how many. Time wasn't on my side, and I had lost a lot of it wallowing. It was time to move.

I pulled my phone and quickly dialed my Aunt Carol's number. It didn't even ring, she answered so fast.

"Oh my god, Scarlett I just saw the news."

"I don't have time that, Aunt Carol," I cut her off. I knew what came next anyway, the apologies about not calling and about what had happened to my father even though it was ages ago. It was like whenever Carol saw me, all she saw was my grief and pain. Marrying into a wealthy family that had immunity ties with the governor was something that had spared her from feeling those two things. "I need you to come get my mom, okay?"

"What?"

"Carol, listen to me. I need to know that you're going to take care of her, okay? I know you two have your differences, but she needs a safe place to live and someone to get her meds for her. Don't leave her in this shit apartment in this shit triad, Carol. Please."

I paused to blink back tears. My voice had cracked a bit more on that last word than I had intended it to.

"Scarlett, you're not running, are you?" Carol's voice was nearly a whisper. "You know what they do to runners."

"I know!" My composure slipped from me for a moment before I could reel it back in. My heart was racing as fast as a horse, and it was putting me on edge. "I know," I repeated more calmly. "Just, please promise me you won't leave her here."

There was silence on the other line for a moment before Aunt Carol sighed, "Scarlett. You know I won't. But-"

"Thank you. That's all I needed to know." I cut her off and ended the call before she could slide anymore words into the conversation.

I slung my duffel bag around my shoulders and scurried out into the living room. My mother sat in the living room. She looked up at me, and her face was streaked with tears. The heavy, dark circles underneath her eyes made it obvious that she had depleted her already fading energy on crying to hard.

"Oh! Scarlett, you're home!" She smiled warmly. "I'm so glad to see you." She spoke slowly, and her words slurred together.

Another episode.

She had them from time to time when her body was at its most fatigued. Moments of lapsed memory. Sometimes they were mild, and sometimes she didn't even know who I was. It hurt my heart to see her like this, but I knew it was for the best.

I had to leave. I had to get out and to lay low until this all blew over. I couldn't let the trials take me. I knew if she was well enough to comprehend that, she would understand. She would have told me to go. I knew Carol would take care of her. She was rich, and her husband had ties that granted his household immunity from the purge. When this was all a distant memory and the entire city wasn't out looking for me, I would come back and take her with me too. I heard California was a pretty good state to be human in; the trials didn't even exist there. We could be safe; I could work, and maybe we could even afford treatment for her.

I had to do it. I had to.

"Yeah, mom, I'm home," I smiled.

"Just in time to help me to bed. I'm so tired." She hung her head, nearly falling asleep in her wheelchair.

"Yeah, I know, mom." I wheeled her into her room and helped her into her night gown. I knew that the clock was ticking, and every second that passed was another second that I should have been farther away from her, but I couldn't just leave her. Not like this.

I pulled the covers over her and sat on the bed beside her.

She looked at me, and her pale blue eyes had meaning behind them. She smiled warmly and laid her hand on mine, but I knew somewhere deep inside of her, she knew what was going on. A piece of her remembered. I couldn't leave her without any explanation.

"I love you, mom." A tear slid down my cheek.

"I love you too, Scarlett. More than anything in the world." She closed her eyes.

"I'm leaving for a while, but Aunt Carol is going to take care of you, okay?" It took every ounce of strength I had to keep my voice from quivering.

"I miss Aunt Carol," she mumbled softly as she slid further into sleep.

"I know." I wiped my tears from my face. "But don't get too used to her mansion and maids, okay? I'm coming back, and when I do, you're going to have to live a boring life with little old me."

My mother smiled, and she drifted deeper into sleep. I wanted to crawl in bed next to her like I sometimes did when shit got rough, but I forced myself to my feet and closed her door tightly behind me.

My phone buzzed in my hand, and I brought it to my ear.

"I'm on my way with my driver. We have immunity plates; no one will touch us. Your mom will be safe. You don't have anything to worry about, sweetie."

"Thank you." I hung up. I didn't want to give her even a split second to let her curiosity about my plans slip out. And I definitely didn't want to hear that she was so sorry, or that I was so brave, or that everything would be okay.

The truth was that I'd been summoned. Nothing would ever be okay again.

I slid on my black leather jacket and let my hair down before slipping out the front door and locking it behind me. I wasn't stupid enough to use the front door, not with the half-wit Invicta members that were probably stalking the street at the very moment thinking of all the non-creative ways they could rip me apart for getting them blown with tarragon.

I adjusted my bag on my shoulder, glad that it still held all of our herb-filled weapons. Tarragon was the only thing that seemed to hurt the vamps, short of decapitating them. It was our only chance at a fair fight, and there was no way I was going on the run without it.

I turned to head toward the back door, creeping as quietly as I could, but the apartment door next to ours opened slowly. Mrs. Camino stood in the doorway and leaned against the door frame. She wiped a stray strand of gray hair from her face and took off her glasses.

I liked Mrs. Camino. She was an old friend of my father's, but the look in her eyes made me uneasy. She was afraid; it was written all over her face. And when people were afraid, they were desperate.

"Scarlett, where are you going?" She eyed me suspiciously.

"Late night walk?" I shrugged, frozen in place.

"She pulled out her cellphone and sighed, "I'm sorry, Scarlett. You know what happens when someone runs. It's counted as a death for our triad, and we're shit out of luck. They're including everyone in this purge, Scarlett. We need every chance we can get." She started to dial a number.

Shit.

I broke out in a run and booked it down the stairs. So much for being quiet and going unnoticed. Neighbors on all three floors opened up their doors to see what the commotion was, and once they saw me rushing down the stairs, they knew what was going on. They each pulled out their cellphones and dialed the number for human control.

I would be lying if I said that my feelings weren't hurt. I had lived in the building my entire life. Each and every one of these people had watched me grow up in one shape or form. Everyone watched me care for my mother. Everyone had looked after me in their own way.

And now they were all turning me in for running from the summoning…every single one of them.

The people pleaser inside me was hurting. I hated it when people were upset with me; it was one of the very few things that I had inherited from my mom. But in that moment, my need to stay alive for my mother burned brighter than the hurt of betrayal from people that I almost considered family.

I had to stay alive—for her. That was all that mattered.

A wave of relief swept over me when I made it to the bottom floor. The red exit door was in my sights when someone stuck their foot out, and I was sent spiraling to the ground. My chest collided with the hard ground, and my duffel bag was sent skidding away from me.

"Human control said not to let her get out. We're supposed to hold her down until they get here; they're five minutes out."

No. This isn't how this ends.

Before anyone could hold me down, I scrambled for my duffel bag, shoved my hand inside, and pulled out the handgun that was inside. I quickly rolled on my back and aimed it in every direction. The three men that had been approaching halted, and their hands shot into the air.

They were scared, but they could tell that I was too. And scared with a gun trumps scared without one.

"Everyone just stay back," I winced, pulling myself to my feet. "I don't want to hurt anyone. I just want to live."

I slowly backed toward the exit.

"We want to live too," a woman's voice echoed from down the hall. "You know what they do with runners. You're taking away a chance that we have to win.

30

I saw her point, but it didn't matter. My sense of self-preservation had kicked in.

"I'm sorry," I stuttered before slipping out the bright red door, leaving behind everything and everyone I'd ever known.

CHAPTER 4

As soon as I stepped foot into the back alleyway, the downpour soaked me. I didn't care though because the weather was on my side. Vamps didn't like to go out in the rain or during storms. Their senses were so heightened that they went into overdrive with all the stimulation, but the storm wouldn't save me from my own people turning against me.

I had to admit that was the part that stung the most. I was prepared not to trust a single vampire that crossed my path, or any supernatural for that matter, but now I had to afford the same courtesy to every human that I came into contact with too.

It broke my heart but hurt feelings weren't something that I had time for, so I kept moving.

I quickly made my way through the alley and peeked my head toward the front of the building just in time to see all of the Invicta scum crawl into an expensive car and ride off. Even the big, bad gang members couldn't handle the rain.

I looked both ways before scurrying across the street into another alleyway disappearing into the shadows, and I ran. I ran so fast and so far that by the time I stopped for air, I had no idea where I was. All I knew was that my muscles were upset with me, and my lungs were on fire. I slumped forward and took in gulps of fresh, fiery air. My clothes were soaked to the skin, and my hair was wet and matted. I realized that I had no plan. I had no friends. Aunt Carol was my only family, and I definitely didn't have any experience running from human control.

I took a deep breath and did my best to calm my mind.

What would Dad do?

I racked my brain for a memory of him. It stung that with every day that went on, it was harder and harder to find any. I missed him more than anything in the world, but he was fading from my mind like a good dream. Soon, all that would be left behind would be the warm feeling.

Think, Scarlett. Think!

First, he would get off the streets. Out in the open is no place for a fugitive, especially a trial runner. If they found me, they would drain me of my blood and string my body up in the street like a

33

decoration.

I thought and thought as hard as I could about what my next move should be. I knew that every second I wasted panting and thinking was another second that human control would be on my tail. Another second of my life wasted.

Then a light went off in my mind. I knew where to go.

***

I quickly knocked on the solid oak door, nervously glancing over my shoulders. The walk across the triad was long, and the shiver from the rain was finally beginning to set in. I was freezing. I was exhausted, and above all else, I was scared. I wasn't going to pretend that I wasn't.

I hoped that Aunt Carol would honor her word, and that by now, my mom was in a luxury car on her way to her new life in the suburbs of triad two. Even if I never saw her again, I hoped that she would be well taken care of.

A streetlamp further down the street flickered, and I flinched.

I was vigilant, a little too vigilant, and I started to understand why the vamps didn't like going out in the rain. They probably felt how I felt in that moment. It was exhausting noticing every subtle movement of the rain, anticipating every enemy that could pop out of the woodwork.

Behind the worn-down door, footsteps approached, and I breathed a sigh of relief. I hoped Charlie actually let me in. He owed my father his life, and I was there to collect on the debt.

The door creaked open slowly, and the old man peaked out.

"Scarlett," Was the only word he uttered. He didn't bother to ask what was wrong or why I was on his doorstep at one in the morning. At that point, he already knew I'd been summoned. The entire city did.

"You owed my father a debt. I'm here to collect on it."

Charlie grunted and closed the door in my face.

Well, that didn't go as planned.

I stood in silence on his doorstep. That was it. That was the extent of my plan. I had no back up. I had no other leverage. I had nowhere to go. At that point, I was sure that the entire city was out looking for me, and it was only a matter of time before they closed in. I might as well have sat on the step and patiently waited for H.C. to pick me up.

There was a sliding sound behind the door as Charlie unhinged the chain lock, and the door slowly creaked open.

Oh thank god.

I breathed a sigh of relief and rushed inside. Charlie's small house was exactly how I'd remembered it from all of the barbeques my dad dragged us to there. Not a thing had changed, all the way down to the photos that hung on the walls. He still had the same dingy loveseat, a single armchair, and an old box television. Only the necessities, obviously.

"Thank you so much," I shivered. "I'm sorry to show up like this, but I literally didn't have anywhere else to go. I'm in deep shit."

"I've heard. The whole city has heard." Charlie's once blond hair was completely white now, and his beard matched. His icy blue eyes looked darker, and there was a look of permanent exhaustion woven into his irises.

"I just need a place to change my clothes and get dry. Then I'm leaving the city; the whole god damn state if I can manage. I can't do it, Charlie. I can't let the trials take the life of another person my mom loves. I just can't-"

Charlie held his hand up to stop me, and I was thankful that he did. I was running out of wind, and my lungs still ached from the surprise cardio. I definitely hadn't trained for any of it, unless you counted getting up from the couch and sprinting to the fridge during commercials as a workout; in that case, I would have been an Olympic athlete.

"You don't have to explain yourself to me, Scar. Your dad wouldn't have wanted to lose you to the trials either."

My eyes teared up, but I didn't think he could tell because of how soaking wet I already was. Everyone in my triad said my dad died a hero, but the truth was I tried not to think about the day that we lost him. We told him to stay inside. He knew we were safe because women and children had immunity during the vampire purge, but there were too many men in the triad that were at risk, especially in our apartment complex. Vamps had a tendency to go for the easy prey first: elderly and people with disabilities. That didn't sit right with my dad. All his other resistance buddies were too scared to leave their apartments, but he walked straight into the chaos with a smile on his face. With his tarragon weapons strapped to his back, he kissed me goodnight, kissed my mother goodbye, and that was the last time we saw him alive.

"Yeah," I mumbled.

"The bathroom's down the hall, but you already knew that." Charlie headed up the staircase. "You're free to stay until the morning. That's the best I can do."

"I'll take it. Thank you," I yelled up the staircase, but he had already disappeared to the mysterious top floor, where I had never been.

I sighed and tried to fight the exhaustion that was slowly settling in. I hadn't slept in over 24 hours. If I had known I was going to be the one picked for the slaughter, I would have caught a few more Z's, but you work with what you have.

I closed the bathroom door tightly behind me and twisted the lock. Deep down, I knew that it wasn't going to protect me from anything, but it made me feel better and that was all that mattered.

I shivered as I stepped into the small shower and basked in the warm water. I didn't realize exactly how cold I was until the hot water stung my skin and thawed me out. I let it wash over me in waves, and it slowly brought me back to life. I was feeling more and more like myself.

I dried off and pulled on a warm set of clothes. I stood in front of the giant mirror, and I almost didn't recognize the person staring back at me. She seemed like a distant memory that didn't even feel like a part of me anymore.

I gathered my pack and made my way out of the bathroom. Faint lights shone down from the top floor and illuminated the staircase.

Curiosity beckoned to me. I'd always wondered what was up there, even when I was a kid. But sleep beckoned to me more, so I made my way to the couch, closed my eyes and let myself swim in the darkness.

***

I woke up to Charlie nudging my shoulder.

"Wake up, kid. Come on, wake up!"

My eyes slowly crept open. He stood over me; his eyes were wide and crazy.

"What. What?!" It took a second for my brain to catch up to where I was and what was going on, but when I did, I shot straight up.

Morning light flooded in through the windows, and the panic set in.

"Oh no. How long did I sleep?"

"Too long. An informant just tipped me off that they tracked you down. They're 10 minutes out."

I felt sick to my stomach. Sleeping too long was a rookie mistake when you were running for your life, but I had no idea what the hell I was doing. I had absolutely no experience fighting for my life, and that was just another reason why I'd never make it in the trials. I was what they'd consider just another pretty face, and they'd be right.

"I'm so sorry." I jumped to my feet and grabbed my bag. "I'm leaving. I'll go. Just tell them that I'm already gone, and maybe they'll let you live." I felt horrible that they'd found out where I was. What they did to people that harbored runners was almost as bad as what they did to the runners themselves. Charlie didn't deserve to be wrapped up in all of my bullshit.

"No, wait," Charlie said. The look on his face made me feel like he was trying to hold the words in. Part of him really wanted me to run, but there was another part that couldn't let me just leave. "Follow me." He quickly climbed the staircase.

"Up there?" I was still programmed never to go up the stairs, from years of being scolded as a kid.

"Now, kid! There isn't much time!"

"Right!" I sprinted up the stairs behind him and stopped at the top with my mouth wide open. The entire upper floor was a room full of television screens, weapons, and ammunition.

Charlie loaded me up with weapons and ammo.

"Charlie?" I muttered. "Why are you doing this for me?"

A sad look spread across his face, and he sighed loudly. "The night your father passed, he called me. He said he needed backup. He said it was our duty as members of the resistance to protect those who couldn't protect themselves. But this was before my wife got sick, and I was too afraid to leave her."

The room went silent. I didn't know how to feel.

"I've been beating myself up about it ever since. But now my wife's dead, and so is your dad. I'm just left here with the pain that I was too afraid to do the right thing. I've been trying to hold the resistance together in his honor, but the governor's empire is too much to fight back against. I figured the least I could do was give you a fighting chance.

There was a thundering pound on the door downstairs.

"Human control. Open up!"

I turned to Charlie with fear in my eyes. "Times up."

A somber look fell on his face.

"There isn't a lot of time. But the best gift I can give you is this," he said loudly over the thundering slams of the battering ram against the front door. "You are stronger than you think. Way stronger. Your dad always talked about how tough as nails his little girl was, even when you were in your teens. You got this. I know that no matter what you do, you'll make triad three proud."

I didn't care anymore if he saw the tears roll down my face. His words hit me to the core because I knew deep down that was what my father would have said if he were there. I was still terrified, but now it was a mix of terror and courage. He was right, I had this. I knew what I had to do. I had to surrender and participate in the trials, but I wasn't going to play. I was going to win.

"Thank you for that." I pulled Charlie in for a big hug. He wore the same cologne my father had. I closed my eyes and pretended he was there, hugging me one last time.

At first Charlie tensed up at my touch, but he quickly melted into it and wrapped his arms around me.

"Make us proud," he said.

My legs shook as I made my way down the stairs.

I turned to see Charlie still standing at the top.

"Aren't you coming down? I'm sure if you just tell them I wasn't running, just visiting an old friend before I had to leave, they won't charge you.

Charlie shook his head. "There's too much resistance intel in this house. Too many illegal weapons, and too much info on everyone. If they get their hands on it, what's left of the resistance is as good as gone."

I didn't understand what he meant. They were already here; there was no way of keeping them from it all now.

In front of me, there was a large crash, and the door gave way to the heavy ram, blowing off its hinges. A handful of agents in full swat gear stormed in, and my hands immediately went up in the air.

"I surrender. I surrender!" I yelled. The red sniper lasers that illuminated my chest made me nervous. I slid out of my bag and placed it carefully on the floor. "I'm not a runner. I accept the summons to the vampire trials. I was just visiting an old friend is all."

An agent drug me out by my arm onto the sidewalk and patted me down. Nearby, a black government vehicle sat running, and they shoved me inside.

"Take her to the manor," the agent said through his mask. Before he closed the door, I heard a call come over the radio.

Multiple weapons found on site. It looks like a-

The call was cut off by a deafening *boom,* and all the windows in the house blew out. Debris and ash flew everywhere.

"No! Charlie!" I screamed.

"Go, go, go!" The agent closed the door, and the car sped off. I turned around and watched as the burning house got further away.

The last tie I had to triad three, gone forever.

CHAPTER 5

I sat quietly in the backseat for what felt like forever. My tears had dried, and all that was left was a hollow feeling. The only people I cared about in triad three, the only people that I even thought were worth fighting for, weren't there anymore. I felt hollow and numb, the exact opposite of someone who was willing to fight for their triad. It wasn't fair to the other people in triad three. I was sure that there were decent people there. People worth fighting for. But I wasn't the warrior that they needed, and I didn't want to be.

The car slowly lurched to a halt, and I peered out at the huge manor in front of me. It was the biggest mansion that I'd ever seen, dedicated solely to training trials competitors. Contestants only got a week to prepare before heading to lose their lives, but rumor had it that the week before the trials was the best of their lives, filled with lavish foods, exotic women, and a lot of sex.

What more could a man facing death want?

I wondered what the final week would be like now that women were allowed to compete. Would it still be filled with food and fun and sex?

I shook the thought from my mind. Sex should be the last thing that I thought about. I had to solely focus on surviving, living to see the next day to get back to my mother, and whether or not that happened hinged solely on what happened in the final week.

A female servant emerged from the lavish mansion dressed in a skintight butler costume. It looked more like something that you'd see on a porn video than an actual working uniform, but it validated the rumor about the final week being filled with exotic women. She had long brown hair that went all the way down to her butt, and the suit hugged her curves perfectly. If I were a man, I probably would have gone crazy to get my hands on her too, but I wasn't. And I didn't go there to have mind blowing sex or gorge myself on extraordinary last meals. I was there to train, learn how to fight, and come out of the trials on top so that I could make it out of the nightmare that I was forced to live through.

The woman opened the car door and motioned for me to get out.

"Scarlett from triad three?" she smiled.

"That's me," I said awkwardly.

"This way," she shut the door and ushered me forward.

She led me into the mansion, and I did my best not to look awestruck, but it was hard. It was the biggest house that I'd ever seen. A breathtaking chandelier stood in the entryway, full of crystals that caught the light just right, sending sparkling light beams scattering across the room. Inside the entryway was a fireplace that blazed brightly. The heat was comforting and coerced me into letting my guard down. I could feel my shoulders relax and the tension leave my muscles.

"Do you like it?" the woman smiled.

"Yes. It's beautiful." I had to admit it. I'd never seen anything like it in my poverty-stricken life. It was the kind of thing you saw in movies but never actually thought you'd get to experience.

"My name is Veda, and for the next week, I'm going to be your personal servant. I'm in charge of giving you anything you like." Her eyes shifted up my body. "And I do mean anything." She grazed her fingertips from my wrist all the way up my arm before I intercepted it and let it loose.

"Thanks, Veda, but you're barking up the wrong tree. Can you show me to my room please?" A look of disappointment stuttered across her eyes, but it was fleeting, and she was back to her normal self.

"Of course. Right this way." She led me through the entryway which opened up into a grand foyer with a skylight ceiling.

The house was way bigger on the inside than it looked from the street. So much so that it didn't even remind me of a house anymore; it reminded me of a luxury hotel. She led me through the marble hallways and gave me a tour of all the amenities that I could use at my leisure. There was a gym, a movie theater, a spa, a training room, and a grand dining hall that she said we were required to eat dinners in with the governors every night at five o'clock.

My stomach churned at the thought of even having to be in the same room as the vampire rulers. Couldn't they just let us train to meet our deaths in peace? Why all the mind games of having to look them in the eyes for an hour every night?

"And this will be your room for the duration of your stay." She led me into a large room that reminded me of a hotel suite.

The bed was the biggest I'd ever seen, like two king sized beds molded into one. It had an elaborate golden canopy that hung over it, with a vintage bathtub right next to it. All of the walls were covered in floor to ceiling windows that overlooked the steep canyon that the house was perched on.

"Oh! Ummm, hello?" I finally noticed a harem of naked women perched on my bed and quickly averted my eyes awkwardly out the window.

"She's not interested, ladies, you're free to go." Veda waved her hand.

The naked women whined in disappointment before sulking out the door.

"You guys were really prepared for a man, weren't you? Got

any harems of sexy men waiting around?"

Veda laughed. "Unfortunately, no. You were the only woman selected this year, and it was a surprise to everyone."

"Figures. Women get the short end of the stick," I groaned. "They're not like- slaves or anything, are they?"

"No! Of course not. As jobs go, they actually enjoy theirs. They chose to do it themselves, and the work is...fun. Let's put it that way," she smirked. "And they treat all of us really well here actually. We're like their beloved pets. It beats being stuck in triad three, living in poverty, trying to scrape by to feed a family."

I nodded. I got it. And why shouldn't women be empowered to embrace their dark and sexy sides whenever they pleased, even when it benefited them and got them out of poverty. It was what my Aunt Carol did and look where she was now—immune from the vampire purge.

I wished that I would have spent more time giving that dark sexy side of me time to prowl and explore. If I had known that my life was going to be cut short at the age of twenty, I probably would have, but you live, and you learn.

"Wait, So I was the only woman selected this year?" My mind finally processed what she had said.

"Yeah. Didn't you watch the rest of the summoning?" Veda eyed me.

"Well, I kind of went numb when they said my name so..." I trailed off, but she understood.

"Your trainer will be here in an hour, but you're free to roam about the house as you please until then." With that, she turned and exited the room.

I stood in the empty room for a while, lost in my own thoughts.

So, I'm really the only girl they chose. Maybe I can use that to my advantage.

Maybe the dark and sexy side of me still had a chance to come out and play. After all, a bunch of men facing their deaths are likely not to be on their best game. When they see me, a beautiful, helpless girl, there's no way that they won't underestimate me. Maybe I could use that to my advantage. Anything that helped me live for a day longer was a day closer I was to seeing my mother again. I was willing to spin it any way I needed to in order to come out on top.

I paced the room getting a look at everything it held. The closet was full of men's suits.

Typical. I snorted. The more I thought about it, the more it felt like the decision to add women to the trials was a last-minute decision. It felt sloppy, and not thought through. If they had known for a while that they were going to add women to the sadistic game, they would have at least taken the time to tailor it to them. Male servants, female clothes, the works. But something about this didn't feel right. It made me wonder what the governor's true reasoning behind it was. Something felt fishy, and I was the type of person that couldn't let an idea go once it entered my mind. Before I knew it, I had already made my mind up. I was going to spend the week training harder than I'd ever trained before, but also digging up as much dirt as possible on the real reason why women were suddenly chosen as contenders- and why I was the first and only one chosen. It felt unnatural, almost staged.

I moved from the closet to the bathtub, running my fingertips along the smooth edge as I walked. I stopped at the bed and admired the craftsmanship of the frame. The four bedposts that held the golden silk were solid gold and intricate leaf designs crawled their way up them.

I couldn't resist the urge to faceplant into the soft comforters and rolled around on the bed. IT was so soft and so plush that I almost didn't want to leave it, but there was more of the house that called to be explored. I didn't know how much time I had before the other competitors started arriving, and I wanted to relish in being one of the only people there.

I found my way back into the marble hallway and wandered for a while. I eyed up every intricate painting that clung to the wall and was shocked to see actual originals of famous painters' works like Picasso. They must have cost a fortune, but then again, I doubted that the governors worried much about money with a house like this dedicated solely to people that they intended to kill.

I wondered for a moment what their houses must have looked like if their disposable ones looked like this.

I turned a corner, collided directly with someone, and spiraled to the floor.

"Hey! Watch where you're walking…" the man stopped when he realized who I was.

I looked up at him from the floor, and I immediately knew who he was. Drax Smith, the governor's only son, also known as triad three's royal bad boy. I had seen him enough in the news for his incessant partying to know who he was at first glance. Even from the floor I could see why they called him a playboy; he fit the mold perfectly. He had the chiseled chin and the body to match. His face was perfectly arranged down to the dimple in the middle of said chiseled chin. His eyes were a deep shade of brown that matched his perfectly styled hair. There was just something about Drax that gave off a vibe that women couldn't ignore. I couldn't lie, I was feeling it too, even laying on the floor with a massive headache from the impact of the fall.

He was holding a martini in one hand and a completely naked woman clung to the other arm. I climbed to my feet and quickly sized him up. I doubted that he would kill me; he was wearing too nice of a red velvet suit. It wasn't the kind I imagined blood would come out of easily.

"You're her, the female contender, right?"

I nodded. As hard as I tried, I couldn't get my brain and my mouth to work together.

"Wow, they really picked out a good one." He devoured me with his eyes, and I hated that it did something for me, seeing him look at me like that. I was sure he'd looked at a hundred other women the exact same way, possibly even just that morning. But something about the way he looked at me so hungrily made me feel like that dark and sexy part of me was ready to finally make her debut.

"You want to come back and join us?" He raised a brow and

motioned to the woman who still clung to his arm.

I shook my head no, still silent.

"Suit yourself." He pulled out a small packet filled with light blue powder, put one end in his nose and sniffed. With that, they turned and continued down the hallway.

"Does she know how to talk?" I heard him murmur to the woman followed by an unbearable cackling.

Ice for sure. It's sad, most vamps are probably on the stuff.

I would have kicked myself for how stupidly I almost fell for his vamp tricks. He was probably coercing me the entire time. There was no way I could have been attracted to one of them. I despised them down to the very pit in my soul. I couldn't possibly even consider sleeping with one.

The thought was enough to ease my nerves. Everyone knew that vampires had the ability of coercion, convincing humans of anything that they wanted. Sure, the power had its limits, but without the herb tarragon in my system, I was defenseless. God knows what Drax could have made me do to him if he had wanted to.

After everything that had happened, I suddenly remembered my trainer was going to arrive soon and hurried back to my room while I tried to rid my mind of anything even remotely related to Drax Smith.

CHAPTER 6

I waited patiently, perched on the bed with my hands folded in my lap. I hated it because it gave me time to actually process what was going on. I wanted to find something to occupy my brain, but I was afraid that if I roamed the halls, I'd run into Drax again, and I didn't like the way he made me feel. I didn't like seeing the vampires up close; it made them seem more human.

It was easier to hate them from afar. I liked it that way.

There was a sturdy knock at the door. Before I could welcome them in, the door opened, and in walked a man. He was short but he made up for it in muscles. His skin was dark and sun kissed, and his eyes were weathered and tired. If I had to guess, I would have put him at about my father's age, only because of the way steaks of white kissed the roots of his dark brown hair.

"Are you my trainer?" I felt stupid for asking such an obvious question.

"I guess I am now," he sighed, which didn't make me feel any better about the situation. "Listen kid, I'm going to be straight with you. I sympathize. I'm from triad three too; it's rough there. You already have to overcome more than the chumps from the other triads just because of that. But you're a girl too. And a supposed runner. No other trainer would take you for whatever combination of all of those things. What a lot of people don't know is the trainers play the game in a way too. When the contender is killed, they kill the trainer too. We have a lot riding on this."

I clenched my teeth together and forced myself to nod. I didn't know that was a stipulation of the game too, but it made sense. They wanted to manipulate as many humans as they could at once, instill as much fear as they could because fear leads to obedience.

"So, I need to know right now, are you in this? Like in it, in it? Because I love a good underdog story myself, and if you're willing to do this, then so am I."

I had to stop for a moment and ask myself the question. Was I really in it? Did I really want to win? If not, I could always blunder the first round and get myself killed right away. Was fighting just prolonging the inevitable.

"That look on your face isn't as promising as I would have hoped, but I'll give you time. There's a lot of shit going on, and I can't even imagine being in your shoes. So, we'll start with something small today, and when you figure out whether or not you're going to treat this as a battle or a suicide mission, we'll plan our next moves."

I nodded again. The poor guy probably thought I didn't know how to talk, but he was right. There was a lot going on, more than I could process. And the truth was, I didn't even really know what I wanted. I didn't know if I wanted to give it my all, or to fade into the background and let whatever happened happen.

"Alright, the first lesson for the day is that presentation is everything, especially because you're the only woman on the roster. You need to decide if you're going to let that be an advantage or a disadvantage."

"What do you mean?"

"I mean, you're in a house full of men, probably arrogant, cocky, sexist ones. By default, they're going to underestimate you. You can use that as an advantage, use your contender outfit to distract, then go in for the kill.

He turned to the doorway and motioned for someone to come in. A few moments later, Veda returned with a few other helpers with arms full of clothes, gowns, and armor.

"The Vampire Trials are a mind game; they always have been, and when it comes to men, it's easy for them to have one thing on their minds."

As I browsed over the beautiful clothes, I got where he was

going.

"Dress to distract, and you dress to kill."

I smirked. He was right. It was genius. Most of the people there already saw me as just a pretty face; why not give them something pretty to look at, and when they let their guard down, give them a taste of what I'm really made of?

"What do you suggest?" I raised a brow.

He could sense the growing excitement inside of me and that made him feel better about his choice to work with me. Maybe there really was an underdog inside of me ready to prove everyone wrong. I had to win. I couldn't let this steal another person from my mother.

"Every contender has to choose a battle suit; it's like their signature outfit that they'll wear during the trials, something that sets them apart from the rest but also works to their advantage. I'm suggesting—and hear me out fully—this."

He reached in the pile and pulled out a skimpy set of armor that looked like it belonged in a porn video along with Veda's maid suit.

I opened my mouth to protest the fact that the *armor* didn't cover a damn thing and shouldn't be considered armor at all, but he held a finger up shushing me.

"I know, it's a shitty set of armor. In a fight, all it'll cover is your damn nipples and a handful of skin, *but* this is a weapon in and of itself. It wows, but it also distracts. It sends a sexy warrior message that everyone has to double take at. And in the few seconds they take to double take or figure out what the hell you were thinking choosing this, or even just process that you're wearing clothes,

55

you pounce. You train your ass off this week with me; you become deadly, and you learn to use those double take seconds to pick them off one at a time."

Again. Genius. Part of me didn't vibe with using my body to lure men to their deaths, but the other part of me knew that it was mine to do what I pleased with. Why not use my curves to help me survive.

"I'm in."

The trainer's face lit up, and I could tell he wasn't lying about rooting for the underdog. He loved a challenge, and I was about as challenging as it got. I barely knew him, but I prided myself in my ability to read people, and I could tell that if anyone was able to turn me from a train wreck into a lethal masterpiece it was him.

"If they want mind games, we're going to give them the ultimate one. During the day, you're going to play the part. A ditsy, sexy woman who isn't taking any of this seriously. No training, no game planning; it might even help if you sleep with a man or two."

"What?" I said, stunned.

"Do you want to go all the way to the finals or not?"

He was right. Drastic times called for drastic measures.

"From the outside, you're going to tick all of the boxes that would set you up for failure. Live it up in the house, party, do whatever you have to do that would make people think that you're nothing more than a star struck girl who isn't going to make it past phase one. Use your sex appeal to your advantage; it'll pay off when the trials begin. People will make allowances for you, think that they're doing you a favor by making things easier for you, and that's when you show them what you're made of. We'll train at night and early in the morning in secret, but the training is the easy part. You have the hard part of convincing them that you're harmless. Nothing more than a pretty face swimming in a pool of testosterone."

I sat quietly trying to process everything that he said. I was at least glad that I'd gotten him as a trainer, even if it was as a last resort. I had no doubt in my mind that every other person would have pushed me to the side and disregarded me.

"I didn't catch your name," I realized.

"It's Vincent, but you can call me Vinny."

I smiled and nodded.

"Alright, the dinner is at five tonight. First impressions are the most important, so make sure you knock it out of the park. I'll meet you back here at one in the morning, and we'll start your first training session." With that, Vinny turned and left the room, closing the door tightly behind him.

An eerie silence fell over the room, and I was left perched on the bed drowning in a pile of designer clothes and makeup. I was still trying to process everything that he had said. Hell, I was trying to process everything that was going on. What he said made sense. Men had been underestimating women since the beginning of time; it wasn't new. But using that to my advantage was a concept so foreign in the society that I lived in that my brain could hardly register it.

Dinner is at five, and it's nearly three. I better get to work.

I filled the vintage bathtub with hot water and slid inside. It was euphoric to finally give my muscles permission to relax, and in the suite, I felt like a queen sitting in her palace ready to build her empire. I took a deep breath and let the empowerment wash over me. It was the exact feeling that I needed to hold on to and channel whenever I needed it. As I soaked, I had an epiphany.

No one at the trials really knew who I was. Every time I met someone, they were meeting me for the first time. I could create any version of Scarlett that I liked, and they would just be forced to accept it as the *real* me because they didn't know any better.

The more I thought, the more confidence I had that this could work. For the first time since I'd been summoned, I felt like I actually had a shot at winning and making it out alive, for my triad and for my mother.

I felt hopeful, and hope wasn't something that I had come across in a long time.

I forced myself from the warm bath and dried myself as I perused the selection of designer gowns. My eyes settled on a red glitter dress with a slit up the front. It gave off strong Jessica Rabbit vibes, and in that moment, I couldn't think of a better example of a sex symbol. It was bright; it was show stopping, and it was a first impressions dress. I fought with it, trying to shimmy it over my butt and stuffing my boobs into it. It was skintight, but I didn't mind because my curves were the best part of my body. The dress highlighted them just right. The slit traveled up my leg and rested at my upper thigh, leaving just enough skin to entice and just enough room for the imagination. I found a pair of red heels to match, and my fingers managed to feel out a diamond necklace in the mound of fabric. I held it up to the light in awe of its beauty. It was easily worth more than most people in triad three made in an entire year at their dead-end job assignments, and I was about to wear it around like it was nothing. I put it on, grabbed the makeup, and headed to the golden encrusted mirror that clung to the wall. I coated my lips in a dark shade of red lipstick, brushed the curls in my hair just right, and threw on some mascara and eyeliner. I stood in the mirror, stunned. I didn't even recognize myself, and I couldn't tell if I loved it or hated it.

It was show stopping for sure. If I were a guy, I probably would have jacked off to myself. All I could do was hope that it had the same effect on the other contenders.

I took a final look in the mirror. This was me.

Scarlett 2.0.

CHAPTER 7

By the time that Veda was sent to fetch me for the elaborate dinner with all the contenders, I was perfectly poised. My lips were plumped, my lashes were long, and the wing of my eyeliner was sharp enough to kill. I had to admit that I'd missed getting dressed up and lavishing myself with perfect hair and makeup. I had enjoyed it when I was in my teens, but when my father passed away and I became the sole caretaker of my mother, my hobbies had to take a back seat.

I forgot how good it felt to get all dolled up. How empowering it felt to be in charge of how I looked. How good I felt when I had time to myself, solely to devote to self-care. It was therapeutic really.

I stood in the mirror and stared at the finished product. My bright red lips, flawless curls, and sexy red dress were definitely show stopping. Hell, if I saw me walking from across a room, I'd stop and stare.

But while it was fun to get to spend time on myself, it would have felt a hell of a lot better if it weren't for such a messed-up reason. The expensive dress and lavish makeup were all basically funded with blood money, and I was drenched in it. I had gotten so lost in enjoying it that I almost forgot the real point of it all—to win this sick and twisted game. It turned out in order to do that, I had to be even more sick and twisted than the other competitors.

But was I capable of that? Would they believe all of this?

Veda must have read my mind from across the room. Her girl senses were going off. I could tell by the way her face softened as she stood leaning against the doorway. She knew the struggle of what I was feeling. I was sure that every woman had at some point in their lives.

She made her way to me and glanced at the both of us together in the mirror. Standing next to one another, we both looked like we could have been the stars of a hit porn film. *Sexy maid meets Jessica Rabbit.*

"All it is, is a part to play. You're an actress, and this is your debut role. The only thing standing between you and that Oscar is yourself."

I perked up at her words. I hadn't thought of it like that.

"You decide. Is this going to be a million-dollar movie or a budget film?" She raised a brow at me, and her brown eyes sparkled. For a second, I wondered what her story was. What brought her here, a human called to play among the vampires.

She was right. Every time I met a person here, it was for the first time. Sure, I felt like a fraud. I knew that this wasn't me, but they didn't. I was in charge of what version of Scarlett they got, and tonight, they were getting the sexual goddess.

I smiled back and fixed my lipstick in the mirror one last time.

"You ready, Scarlett?" Veda called form the hall.

"Yeah but call me Scar," I smirked.

Veda smirked back understandingly and nodded.

***

It was obvious that I was the last to make it back to the grand dining room by how loud the laughter and drinking was. When you take over a dozen men, with over half of them in their last days, add booze, food and exotic women, what you have left is pure chaos. As we approached the hall, it became more important.

"Uhh- Am I late?" I asked nervously over the commotion. I was finding it hard not to trip and speak coherently at the same time. I hadn't worn a pair of high heels in ages, and my feet were making sure that I knew it.

And the dress was so tight that it was almost hard to breathe.

"Fashionably," Veda smiled. "I wanted to give you the best shot at a grand entrance that I could. You only get one shot at that you know."

It made sense. But why was she helping me? What did she gain?

Don't tell me they slaughter the handmaids too if I don't win.

At that point, I wouldn't have put anything past the ruthless governors. They were merciless. I doubted that the slaughter of their help was beneath them.

We made it to the entryway of the dining hall and stopped at the top of the small set of stairs that lead down into the eating area. In front of us was a long metallic dining table covered with more delights than I cared to count. There were hams and roasts and fruits and rolls—pretty much everything from that pyramid that they're forced to teach you in school that no one ever uses again. Around the table were the contenders, three from each triad, excluding three of course. Splashed amongst them were scantily clad women who hung from their arms and grasped their chests, no doubt their bed mates for the duration of the stay at the manor. My breath stuttered as my eyes slid down the table and fell on Drax. He was hard to miss in his bright red suit. I hadn't expected to see him at a dinner that didn't involve illegal drugs or sex; then again, the girl that was all over him was probably there to fix that last part.

Oh no. My eyes fell on who sat beside Drax: Colt and Finn Rivera. The vampire playboy twins who were set to inherit triads two and one. My stomach churned at the sight of all of them together.

What the hell are they all here for? My entire life, nearly every media story surrounded them. They were the crowned princes of New York City, and up until now, all they ever delighted themselves in was women, magical drugs, and senseless killings. I supposed that it made sense for them to start to show at least a little interest in the family businesses of governing before they got their silver spoons ripped from between their fangs.

And finally, at the end of the table sat the three governors. Surprisingly, they were throwing back beers too, laughing along with the others. It was odd to see them in such an unprofessional setting. All the times I had ever seen them on the television, they were so somber and cold. Now, if I hadn't known better, they almost would have blended in with the crowd. They could almost pass for something other than blood sucking sociopaths with a power complex.

I took a deep breath. I needed to chill. At that moment, *Scarlett's* political activist side was crawling its way out, but that wasn't what I needed. I needed Scar, and her carefree sex appeal.

I'm Scar now. I'm Scar now. I'm Scar, I repeated in my head.

Veda cleared her throat loudly over the commotion, and everyone looked in our direction.

"Introducing, Lady Scar," she said with a bow. She turned to make her way back down the hallway that we had come from, and she made wide eyes at me to say something—do anything other than stand there like a fool. A series of whoops, whistles, and cat calls emerged. I imitated my best sexy stair walk and let the dress and the shoes together do something magical to my curves. It was working; even the governors had a twinge of interest in their eyes.

"Oh please, don't make all that fuss over me, boys," I did my best to make my voice sound as smooth and sexy as possibly. I flashed a coy smile. "Now which of you gentleman is going to give up his seat for the lady?" I raised a brow.

Nearly all the contenders raised their hands into the air. They were practically tripping over each other just for the chance to offer up their seat for me, to win points hopefully redeemable for a rendezvous in my bed, no doubt. I didn't mind all the fuss; it was trying to keep a straight face when these men acted a fool that was the hard part.

"Eenie, meenie, minie," I made my way around the table and ever so lightly ran my fingertip over each one's shoulder. "You," I stopped at an ashy blonde with a chiseled chin and arms to match. "What's a lady got to do to get your seat?" I kissed the side of his face lightly, leaving a bright red kiss mark behind in its place.

"Oh nothing, honey. I have the best seat in the house for you right here," he winked and pulled me into his lap.

I giggled and played along, but inside, I had to keep myself from gagging at his response. Around me, the other players ogled me. I even got a passing glance from Drax, Colt, and Finn every once in a while. It wasn't my favorite imaginary role, and if I had been given the choice, I would have been as far away from any of it as possible, but given the circumstances, I was doing pretty well at my self-induced undercover mission.

I'd finally convinced the blonde guy to get his ass out of the chair and let me sit in it freely when the waiters finally pulled the plates from the table and started to file in with the dessert dishes. I thought that I was impressed with the dinner they served, but the dessert selection made the dinner look like the McDonald's dollar menu. There were cakes, pies, and cookies that I didn't even know existed. I didn't know where to start, and just as I was going to reach for a cookie, I stopped.

Mind games. That's all the trials were. And I almost didn't see it, but the mind games didn't start when the competition bell rang and the trials began. It was more sadistic than that. For the contenders, those mind games started the second the governors picked our names from the running and declared us officially summoned. Out of the corner of my eyes, I glanced down at the Governors. They mumbled amongst themselves, but one, the governor of triad two, eyed me cautiously before leaning in to whisper something.

The mind games had already started, and the first was pumping us full of decadent food and sweets, slowly eroding our health and fitness right before they unleashed us into a *to the death* killing match against one another.

"Excuse me?" I held my hand up, catching a waiter's attention. "Could I just get a small salad please? I'm trying to watch my carbs." Out of the corner of my eye, I saw the governor's eyebrow raise.

Shit. Recover, Recover. You can't let them know you're onto the games they're trying to play.

"All the weight I gain always goes right to my boobs," I lied. "And I'm trying to keep them just the perfect size." I ran my fingers over them, and the guys around me did their best not to let me know that they were mesmerized by the simple words.

They stared, but I didn't care. Whatever got them less focused on my brain and the actual threat that I could pose was worth it.

I stuck it out through the rest of the meal, even though it almost hurt to act so shallow for so long. It took so much energy to put on the show that by the end of the dessert course, my cheeks hurt from smiling, and my eyes watered from all the fake laughing I forced myself to do.

"Well, boys," I feigned a yawn. It's about time for me to retire to my room. A girl's got to get her beauty sleep," I smirked. It was exhausting, but the longer I stayed in "character," the easier it was to be Scar, and the men were eating it up.

Drax eyed me from across the room suspiciously. "Let me escort you. A pretty lady like you shouldn't have to walk alone." A smug smirk spread across his face, and I shuddered internally.

"I would love that."

Not.

I got up from the table, and being the first to leave, all eyes were on me. Drax met me around the other side of the table and held his arm out. I obliged and tangled mine with his, and we made our way back to the room.

My mind was racing, and my thoughts didn't know which way to go.

What does he want with me? He wouldn't dare kill me, would he? No, he wouldn't go through all that trouble.

"Well, this is my stop," I smiled meekly. "I'm so tired." I stepped inside and tried to shut the door, but he wedged his designer shoe inside.

I looked up, and our eyes met. This close to him, I realized that I'd never seen a shade of brown as deep as those eyes. They say eyes are the window to the soul, but that couldn't be true because blood suckers couldn't have souls. Could they?

"Won't you invite me in?" he smiled, and his fangs glistened. I didn't want to admit that something twinged inside of me at the sight of the gorgeous playboy practically begging to be close to me.

"Sure," I forced myself to smile.

What's a few minutes to calm his suspicion? I reasoned.

He stepped inside and closed the door tightly.

"Right, so how about you tell me what the hell you think you're doing?"

CHAPTER 8

I stood frozen and stared at Drax with a blank look on my face. My heart raced, and my palms were sweaty. There were probably hundreds, if not thousands, of women who would have killed to be in my position. Locked in a room alone with the infamous Drax, in a sexy red dress with no one else to pull his attention but me.

But I hated it. It was the last place I wanted to be.

"I- I don't know what you mean." I tried to play stupid, but the look on his face told me he wasn't falling for it. Something told me that Drax, son of the most ruthless and maniacal triad governor, wasn't exactly what everyone thought.

Drax sighed and unbuttoned the top button of his blood red blazer. "I didn't want to resort to this, but it looks like I have to.

"Uhm, what are you doing?"

With each button he unfastened, a little more of his chiseled chest came to light. A suit with no shirt underneath, classic playboy fashion. I averted my eyes and awkwardly found a spot on the ceiling to stare at.

"What's the matter? Are you shy?" He ripped his coat off, and it crumpled in a pile in the corner. He slowly moved closer, inch by inch, and I didn't know how to feel. I hated to admit that part of me was attracted to him, just like every other girl that was forced to watch him grow up in the spotlight of the media in triad three. I hated that inside of me, seeing his body did something for me. I was turned on by a vampire. A monster.

The other part of me knew that no matter how attractive he was, it didn't make up for the fact that he was a killer, probably a cold blooded one at that.

"Don't you want to have fun?" Drax was so close now that I could smell whatever delicious designer cologne he'd lathered himself in. His breath was warm against my skin. An electricity hung in the air; it was a magnetic feeling that pulled me to him, and I hated it. It had to be a vampire power, some way of him obliging me to feel this way. It couldn't be real.

I remembered what Vinny said. I had to make it real, believable. I couldn't let anyone catch on to the game that I was playing, otherwise it could mean game over for me when the trials started.

That meant I had to make sacrifices. I pulled Drax in for a kiss, and a wave of electricity flowed through me. It wasn't in the metaphorical sense, either. It was an actual electric shock that sent shivers down my spine and pulsated through my veins. I pulled away and looked into Drax's eyes.

He smirked.

"So that's it. Your trainer told you to play the part of the dumb, sexy chick to throw everybody off your trail. Smart."

"Wait what? What just happened?"

Drax made his way to his blazer in the corner and slid it back on, and I stood in the doorway as confused as I'd ever been.

"You obviously don't know very much about Vampires, or you'd know we each have a special ability. A power, if you will. And mine is being able to extract information about people through touch, and you just gave me everything that I need."

My fists balled up. "That's a little bit of an invasion of privacy, don't you think?" A slow burning anger bubbled up in my chest. Just another thing that the vampires thought they could take from me freely without my consent.

"Eh." Drax shrugged and flopped himself onto my bed. "If you got it use it, right? Isn't that what you're doing with your body? It puts you at an advantage. So why not use it?"

I stared at him blankly, unsure if I was offended or if it made sense. Either way, the dress I was in was strangling me, and my makeup was stinging my eyes. The ruse was up with him anyway, so I went to the sink and washed my face.

"You can leave now," I dismissed him with a wave of my hand.

"Actually, I'd like to stay. I've never met a girl before who wasn't very obviously throwing herself at me. You truly want nothing from me, and nothing to do with me. You're like a Unicorn. A mythical creature."

"What exactly is it that you want from me, again?" I rolled my eyes at his poor attempt at flattery. It probably did sting to be coddled for your whole life and finally meet someone who didn't bow to kiss your feet when you walked. "Don't you have any other girls that you can harass? It looked like there were plenty waiting for your beck and call. Why don't you go bother one of them while I work on trying to survive?"

"Join the club," he mumbled as he watched me wipe the mask of makeup from my face.

"Excuse me?" I spun around. The anger that was once slowly burning inside my chest nearly erupted into a wild blaze that threatened to engulf anything it touched in its burning touch. "What's wrong? Is your crown of vampire privilege too heavy for your little head? Are the shoes you're set to fill too big for your feet? I'm so sorry. You poor thing, why don't you go buy another luxury car, or sleep with a few women. I'm sure that will heal your fragile ego." I was seething just at his comment. How dare he even compare his proposed suffering to mine? He was on the top of the food chain, living in a pool of wealth and luxury. I was fighting just to survive.

I stood so close to him now that I could see the glimmer of sadness in his eyes. Before I knew what was happening, he pulled me in for another kiss. Instead of the electric sting I'd felt earlier, this time, I felt a rush of warm energy seep into my body.

I closed my eyes, and a wave of images flooded my mind. I saw Drax as a kid. I knew it was him because he'd been plastered in the media since the moment he was born. He was sad, and he was scared, cowering in a dark room. He still had the same warm chocolate eyes that he did now. I didn't know where he was, but wherever it was, he was terrified. I knew because his emotions swept through my body like they were my own. Suddenly, a door crept open, and a small sliver of light flooded the dark closet that Drax sat in. When the light illuminated his face, I noticed the rapidly healing black eye and cut that sliced across his cheek.

"There you are boy," The governor's low snarl of a voice came from the doorway. "Quite bitching, you're supernatural. It's already healing."

Drax's eyes filled with tears.

"You need to get up and be a fucking man."

I pulled away from Drax's kiss and stared at him. I didn't notice the tears until they started running down my cheeks in warm streams. Drax stared back at me, his face nonchalant.

"Well, I guess you can transfer information through touch too," I mumbled.

"Yeah, I can use any touch. But kissing is so much more fun," Drax smirked. He was slowly going back into his playboy shell. "I just wanted to show you that not everyone's life is as perfect as it seems."

I turned back to the mirror and continued washing my face. I didn't want him to see the change in my eyes.

"Sure, but you're still a vampire. You were born with privilege, and you were born a killer." The words spilled out of my red lips like venom shooting out of a snake's fangs. They weren't aimed to hurt; they were aimed to kill, and once they were out, I didn't regret a single syllable.

My eyes flitted to Drax's face in the mirror behind me for a millisecond. The anger in his eyes told me that they had done their job. I got a sick sense of satisfaction from hurting him. In a sick way, hurting him was like my revenge for my kind. A little dig for humankind against the vamps.

"Well, I'm sorry that I was born a vampire. I didn't ask for this shit," he yelled.

I turned to face him again.

"And I didn't ask to be human, hunted down for sport, and walked all over," I glared at him with fire in my eyes.

"Oh please, humans were doing that to each other long before supernaturals finally came out of hiding. You guys destroyed yourselves centuries ago. You always need someone to hate, someone to blame." The words seeped into my skin. He was right, but that didn't justify anything.

"Well, at least I can walk out in daylight!" I yelled, immediately regretting that I even let the words come out of my mouth.

So much for an intellectual argument.

A laugh erupted from Drax's lips. He laughed so hard that tears ran down his cheeks. He was laughing, the kind of belly laugh you get when you and your friends are together. The kind that you can't stop once it starts. It was infectious laughter, and I hated that it spread to me. I held it in for as long as I could, with my lips clamped tightly together. But it was the kind of laughter that couldn't be caged. It exploded out of me in waves that hurt my sides and tickled my stomach.

I couldn't control it, and neither could he. So there we stood, two different species at war with one another, fighting with laughter in an empty room.

"That's your argument?" Drax said between laughs. "That's the argument you're using to defend mankind's superiority?"

"Shut up." I gasped for air, and the laughter finally settled. The muscles in my face ached, and my sides cramped. I threw myself on the bed and let out a long sigh. Drax laid beside me, but I didn't have the energy to tell him to fuck off anymore.

So we just laid there, feeling the after high of our laughter, panting in silence.

Drax turned to me, and for the first time since I'd ever seen him in a newspaper, there was something different about him. In this light, with a smile on his face, if I hadn't known a single thing about him, I would have sworn we were the same. Not vampire, not human, just people.

I was stubborn like my father. I hated to admit that I was wrong, but maybe there was more complexity to the situation. Maybe it wasn't as black and white as I thought.

I lived in a world where you were either vampire or human. Was it possible to just be a person?

"That was an incredible burn, by the way." His eyes locked in on mine. "But for the record, I have daylight powers. *And* I've never killed anyone. But it's nice that you think I'm that bad ass."

I snorted.

"I never wanted this. Any of it. Most of the time I'm like you, playing a part. The Drax Smith you know is nothing but a role on the television show we call life. Girls, sex, drugs, I fucking hate it all. I live in a world where everybody either wants something from me or wants to kill me. I don't want to be the fucking governor. I don't want to promote the trials, and contrary to popular belief, I *don't* want to kill anyone."

I watched the change in his eyes as he confessed to me. I was good at reading people, and my internal meter told me he was telling the truth.

"Huh. Who knew?" I mumbled.

He was charming, I gave him that. Even for a vampire, he was the type of guy that grew on you, had layers. Maybe he really was just a victim of his circumstances, just like me.

We didn't say another word. We just laid in the bed and wallowed in everything we had said. Turns out, life wasn't fair for a lot of people in ways that I didn't even understand. Who was I if I couldn't admit that I was wrong? What kind of activist would I be if I didn't keep my mind open to new possibilities?

It felt weird, opening myself up to new possibilities. And it scared me. I had spent the last five years letting my feelings about my father's death fester. I needed someone to blame, and the vamps were the easy target. They were easy to hate. Easy to paint as monsters, and I was afraid of what life would be like when I could no longer blindly hate them for it.

But if I was going to die soon, I was going to die with a clear conscience and no unfinished business. Maybe this was the start.

"That's it," I said, breaking the silence. "I've made up my mind. Drax Smith, in Scarlett Johnson's book of life, you are no longer a vampire. You're a person."

CHAPTER 9

I ushered Drax out of my room shortly after our conversation. I was less worried about somebody seeing him coming out of my room and more worried about what incoherent babble might come out of my mouth the longer that he stayed. I was still mourning my loss of hatred for *all* vampires, but I made myself feel better by directing it toward the vampires that I actually knew were shitty—the three governors.

I finally climbed out of my dress and into my bed. No matter how hard I tried, I couldn't stop thinking about what Drax had showed me in the vision and the monster that his father was. Thinking about it made me even more grateful that I had been blessed with a dad who loved me. Even though he was gone, I was grateful to have had him in my life.

I let out a long sigh and rolled over. I wondered what my father would have thought about everything going on in the world today. What he would have said when I got picked. I knew one thing, he always told me to do my best at whatever I wanted to do. Even when it came to school projects. If I didn't want to do the work? Fine. But I had to own up to the grade that I got and do whatever I could in my power to balance it out. I realized that if he were there, he would have given me the same advice.

Johnson's don't do anything halfway, Scarlett. He would say. *You're either all in, or all out.*

As I drifted off to sleep dreaming of his cologne, I decided that was the final straw. I was all in.

***

I was woken up by a soft knock on my door in the middle of the night. Luckily, I was the world's lightest sleeper because it was so faint that I was sure even the vampires wouldn't have been able to hear it.

I opened the door to see Vinny with a smile on his face. "You opened the door! I'm assuming that means that you've decided to grab this thing by the balls," he smiled.

"Definitely not the words I would have used, but if you mean am I ready to go all in, then yes." I rubbed at my eyes sleepily, threw on a light jacket and followed him out the door.

I let out a yawn as we walked down the hallway and toward the training gym that Veda had showed me earlier.

"Yeah, the lack of sleep is going to be the hardest part about all of this for you, kid," Vinny said as he held open the door to the training arena for me. "Train at night and mingle during the day. It sounds a lot easier than it's actually going to be."

Lucky me.

I stepped inside to the large room, and the motion-sensored lights turned on. The room itself was about as big as a basketball court, and four concrete walls framed it. On each wall hung a plethora of weapons, shields, and swords. I'd never seen anything like it in my life. Inside the room there were sparring areas, a boxing ring, treadmills, and weights. It was like an athlete's paradise. I probably would have been more impressed if I was actually even the slightest bit athletically inclined, but it all just looked like a foreign world to me.

"So, tell me your strengths," Vinny said, locking the door to the arena behind him.

"Uhh-" I stared at him blankly.

"Okay, tell me your weaknesses," Vinny sighed.

"Uhh-"

"Okay. Tell me your name. Do you at least know that much about yourself?"

I rolled my eyes, and Vinny smiled.

"I'm serious, kid. You have seven days to prepare yourself for the shit that's about to come your way. Seven days to brace yourself for the trauma you're about to go through. And seven days to determine whether or not you're going to make it out of this mess alive. Do you hear me? This isn't just some high school track meet training. This is some Roman Coliseum type shit. What happens in this room over the next week is what's going to determine whether you get killed or do the killing."

His words shook me to my core. He was right. I guess it just hadn't fully dawned on me that I was going to actually be in the Vampire Trials, a *to the death* battle. At some point, I was going to have to kill somebody at least once, but probably a lot more times if I wanted to live.

Did I have that in me? Did I want to?

"Hey, kid, snap out of it. I see that look in your eye; don't go down the rabbit hole. You could battle yourself over this all day if you let it, so it's best if you just don't think about it for as long as you can. Okay? We'll start small."

I nodded. He sounded like he knew what he was talking about, like he was talking from experience.

"We'll just have to start from scratch and see what we're working with. It's going to be a long night."

We started on the treadmill, which was where we found out that I had the cardiac endurance of a hundred-year-old hospice patient.

"Really? Not even a mile?" Vinny taunted, shocked.

I dismissed him with a wave, panting as I did. I was surprisingly more out of shape than I'd thought, which was already extremely out of shape.

Then we went to the boxing ring to test hand to hand combat. We slipped on the boxing gloves, and Vinny took a few jabs at me. I surprisingly was able to dodge them completely, but when it started getting to my head, I slowed down to smile and took a jab directly to the face. My legs folded in on me, and I spiraled to the ground.

"That actually wasn't half bad. We'll count it as a strong point for you."

"Yipee," I said from the floor coddling my nose.

Then we moved to the weapons testing, which was arguably my favorite part of our entire training endeavor. There were so many weapons that I didn't even know where to begin, but I looked up at them with a glint in my eye, and Vinny caught on to it.

When I was younger, I was a tomboy and went through a weird weapons phase. Totally normal, right?

Looking up at the astounding wall brought back nostalgic feelings of a simpler time, when both my parents were alive, and the world looked big and wonderful, instead of small and scary. I reached up and pulled a samurai sword from the wall. It was a lot lighter than I thought it would have been.

"Oh, we're going right for the kill. Okay," Vinny smiled. He tossed me a protective suit and pulled a matching sword from the wall. I barely got the suit on when he took a swipe at me with his sword, which I barely dodged.

"What the hell! I wasn't even ready!" I yelled.

"Oh, I'm sorry. Be sure to tell your opponents in the trials that you're ready so they know when it's okay to start their attacks.

Okay?"

"That's different," I groaned.

"No. It isn't. You need to learn to always be on your toes. Always expect an attack. Always be on your best. Some of these people are snaky, and even the ones that aren't will be singing a different tune when the trumpet goes off and they realize that it's suddenly everyone for themselves. The only person that can keep you alive is you. Remember that."

I raised my sword and took a half hazard swipe at him, which he dodged, sending me spinning in a circle. My frustration grew, and it made me even sloppier than I already was. I straightened out and took another swipe at him. This time he dodged it so fast that it sent me stumbling forward, and he stopped me with his blade just inches from my neck.

"Dead. Again."

I was getting really sick of training. "All this is doing is showing me all the reasons why I'm probably going to die." I threw the sword to the side and huffed. "You don't think I don't already know that I'm a hot mess with absolutely no survival skills? I do! I might as well be another pretty face; it seemed like I was at least good at that."

Exhausted, I plopped myself down to sit on the treadmill. Vinny crouched beside me, and I averted my eyes to the wall. I didn't want to look at him. I could feel the motivational speech coming on, and right then, all I wanted to do was wallow. I thought I'd earned at least a few minutes of wallowing.

"Look at me, kid."

Here it comes.

"You know what inspired me to become a trials trainer?"

"Something inspirational, I bet," I mumbled quietly.

"My son was summoned five years ago, on his 18th birthday actually. Just old enough to be put in the running, and the unlucky bastard got summoned. He was the scrawny brown kid in school. He had asthma and glasses, and he was picked on constantly. He wanted to drop out and just get a job, but I wouldn't let him. When he got summoned, I begged them to let me volunteer to take his place. I made every call. I wrote every letter, but they wouldn't. He survived four years of high school hell just to be killed in the first round of the trials. For nothing." Tears filled up Vinny's eyes and threatened to spill out onto his cheeks, but he didn't care. It was nice to see a guy so buff and fit and masculine not shudder at the first sign of actual emotions.

"He was the underdog, but no one believed in him. His trainer did a half ass job of preparing him, and he had no idea what he was getting into. We didn't even get his body back for a funeral. It was then that I decided that when the next trials came along, that I would adopt the underdog. The little guy. The person that no one thought in a million years would take the trials by storm. Little did I know that it would be a girl."

"Do you think I can? Take the trials by storm?" I asked.

"I think you got a shot. You got people out there to fight for, okay? Don't throw your towel in just yet. Promise?" Vinny's accent was thick.

"Yeah. I promise."

Vinny held his fist out, and I bumped it with mine. He slid his to the side and pointed his elbow at me.

"It was our secret handshake, but I'll let you borrow it. okay?"

I touched my elbow to his and smiled.

"You're going to be singing a different tune when I kick your ass in this next sword fight," I smirked before throwing my gear back on and grabbing my sword.

We sparred, ran, and trained for three more hours before calling it quits. We said our goodbyes and headed our separate ways down the hall. Every inch of my body ached and screamed, and I was drenched from head to toe in sweat. All I wanted to do was slip into the bath and catch as much sleep as I could before the day's press conferences. It made my stomach turn that the trials were televised, that families were forced to watch as their loved ones were slaughtered. But it made me feel even worse that I had to get glammed up, slide into a skimpy outfit, and pretend to be the *Scar* that the other contenders had come to know. What I wanted to do was get on camera and yell *Fuck* the trials, but that wouldn't have gotten me anywhere.

I was so lost in my thoughts that I hadn't even noticed that I passed my door. The house looked different in the dark, and I lost my way. I back tracked and finally located the clean, white door and walked in. The lights were off, but I didn't care. At that point, all I wanted to do was get out of my sweat soaked clothes and get into the steaming hot bath that I'd started.

I peeled my clothes off layer by layer, and my eyes started to adjust to the room. Something seemed a little off about the placement of the furniture, but I was tired, so I didn't give it much attention and slid into the warm bath.

I let out a soft moan and let my muscles melt into the warmth.

Suddenly, the light flicked on, and I was temporary blinded.

"What? Who's there?" My eyes slowly crept open, and my jaw dropped. In front of me stood Colt, one of the governors' twin sons. He was completely naked from head to toe, and I couldn't pull my eyes from his manhood that hung eyelevel.

"I could be asking you the same thing, darling," he smiled.

CHAPTER 10

Oh my god. Oh my god. Oh my god. It was like my mind froze solid. It refused to work anymore, and it just so happened to freeze with my eyes on his junk. *Just my luck.*

"Would you like to take a picture? It would last longer," Colt laughed.

"Oh my god. I thought this was my room. I'm so sorry," I jumped up from the bathtub, prepared to get out.

Colt looked me up and down. "By all means, please stay."

Oh my god.

I realized that I was sporting my birthday suit and quickly sat back down. I breathed a sigh of relief at the modesty that the bubbles afforded.

Why am I acting so god damn stupid?

My cheeks were on fire, and I knew it was obvious.

"I- I don't know what to do here," I stammered. I was stuck. Jam packed in the middle of the most awkward situation of my life. And it didn't help that he was a gorgeous specimen of a man. Both the twins were.

"By all means, finish your bath," Colt casually strolled back to his bed, climbed under his sheets, and picked up the thick book on his bedside table. "From what Drax tells me, you're cool, so it's okay." He licked a finger and turned a page of his book.

That dick! One soft moment, and he goes out and spreads the word that I'm practically a total fraud.

"What did he say?" I tried to ask casually, but the crack in my voice betrayed my confidence.

"That you two kissed. A lot." He peered over the top of his book and raised a brow over his sparkling blue eyes. His mess of ashy blonde hair stood up over the rim.

"A lot?" I laughed nervously. "I wouldn't say a lot. Did he say a lot?" I stopped myself. I was rambling, and we both knew it.

"He was right. You are cute when you're nervous." Colt smirked, but it wasn't the cocky kind that Drax always wore. It was a short glimpse of his genuine smile, and even from the little tease that I got, I could tell that it could light up a room.

"Are you guys close?" I struggled to change the subject almost as much as I struggled to stop picturing his naked body beneath the comforter.

"Eh," he shrugged. "Growing up with dickwad governor dads will do that to you. They wanted us to be close to *forge the bond of the triad alliance.*" Colt flipped a page. He was very nonchalant about it, which showed the drastic change between Drax and his personalities. Drax had sex and did drugs to deal with his pain. From what I could tell, Colt read books.

My eyes flitted to the stack on the end table.

Lots and lots of books.

Something inside me stirred. Two out of the three playboy princes I'd managed to gear my hate towards were shaping up to be pretty decent people, and it was seriously messing with my head. It's hard to come to the realization that something you'd been taught your entire life might not actually be true.

"This is weird," I sighed. I was too tired to overthink it anymore, and I was too tired to fight the beckon of the hot water to relax. I sat back and let my eyes close. "But I'm probably going to be dead in a week, so you know what? I'm going to roll with it."

There was something about Colt that didn't make my mind raise red flags like Drax. He was so laid back, so nonchalant, that it made me feel less on edge too. And I was naked in front of a complete stranger so that was saying a lot. Colt and Finn were from a different triad than I was, so I hardly ever saw any of the bad news tabloids like I did with Drax.

Their father's a more conservative governor, not as outspoken as the governor for three, so maybe that's why he's so mellow.

"My dad's a piece of shit and had no part in how I turned out," Colt said out of nowhere. "If anything, my revolving door of nannies were to thank for my demeanor."

Oh my god.

"I don't just read books," Colt turned another page. "Your mind is quite interesting actually. The amount of time you've spent just thinking about my junk in the last ten minutes is pretty interesting too." He finally pulled himself from his book and slid his hands behind his head. A smile spread across his face. "I'm glad you liked what you saw, though. Flattered actually."

I wanted to die. Crawl in a hole and literally die of embarrassment.

"So Drax didn't rat me out. You read his mind."

"I didn't have to read it; it was practically screaming. It was utterly impossible to ignore."

Every word that came from Colt's mouth was poetry. It was like a symphony that you could never get tired of listening to. It was obvious he spent most of his time with his nose buried in a book.

My thoughts raced, and I hated wondering whether or not he could hear them.

I hated even more that he was right. I couldn't stop thinking about how he looked naked.

My cheeks burned bright red.

"Would it help you calm down if I got some clothes on?" he asked.

I nodded, completely aware of how idiotic I was coming off as. I turned my head and looked out the window, pretending to be especially interested in the canyon. Behind me, I heard him shuffling around.

"Yes, it's safe to look." he groaned, reading my mind again.

I turned and breathed a sigh of relief at the sight of him in his blue jeans and plain black t-shirt. I could still make out the outline of his manhood through his pants, and I hoped that he couldn't tell.

"Better?"

"Better," I smiled.

The mood in the room stabilized; it was less awkward with only *one* of us in the nude.

Colt sat on the end of the bed and looked at me curiously.

"What?" I asked. His undivided attention made me feel weird, and I wondered what he was looking for. "What!" I asked again.

"Your mind is exceptionally strange," his British accent made it sound like a compliment. "It's like a maze, organized chaos."

"I doubt it's *that* special," I rolled my eyes. "I bet you say that to all the naked women that stumble into your room in the early hours of the morning just to hijack your bathtub."

"Actually I do, but please don't tell the others." Colt smiled and his dimples showed. It was enough to make a girl swoon, but the more that I was at the manor, the more I wondered if I really was attracted to vampires or if I was just getting desperate knowing that I probably wouldn't live to see my next birthday.

"Honestly, though, your mind is like an enigma. Most minds are a mess, thoughts are laying all over the place like trash. I usually can't tell up from down in people's heads, but that pretty little head of yours is different. It's like a maze where the walls are really bookcases. All your thoughts are labeled neatly all in a row, but I can't seem to find my way through. It's incredible really."

It was definitely one of the most unique compliments that I've gotten.

"Well if you're really in my head, tell me my favorite color," I smirked.

"Red."

"Favorite food?"

Chocolate ice cream."

"Favorite person?"

Colt paused.

This is it. I finally got him.

"Your father." he said, to my surprise. "That one was one of the ones that was harder to find. You keep him filed away deep inside the maze. Why?"

His question caught me off guard. He was right. Every day that went on, I found myself thinking of my father less and less. Every day that passed by, the pain of losing him got easier to deal with, but the memories also became more faded.

"I lost him, in the last purge." I shifted my eyes from Colt's, to the bubbles that floated carefree atop the water.

"I'm sorry to hear that," Colt sighed.

I bet you are. It's easy to say when you're a vampire. Part of the problem. The thought of my father started to bring up some of the hatred that I kept locked away, stored deep inside of my heart.

"I know. It's not right, and it's not fair. But I didn't ask to be born a vampire."

"And I didn't ask to be born human, but here we are. You, an honored guest, and me, a prisoner about to fight to the death."

Colt sat quietly. I expected him to have something to say, to defend his kind, or downplay my suffering. Or even have a snippy comeback like Drax, but he just nodded.

"You don't have anything to say?" I snapped. My anger simmered beneath the surface. I had so much pent up that I needed to blow off. I was looking for an argument.

"What does one say when their people have committed atrocities in their name? Were you expecting me to justify it? Because I can't."

My eyes widened. "You don't have an argument?"

Colt chuckled. "Quite the opposite really, I agree. Throughout history, vampires have been monsters. They've enslaved humankind and committed mass murder in the name of vampire kind, and it's sick."

"Oh. Yeah, I'm right," I huffed.

"Not every vampire believes in the invisible cause though, you know," Colt sighed, and my attention perked up. "We live in modern times. There are artificial blood substitutes; there are animals that are edible; there are a lot of different things that vampires can do as opposed to slaughtering humans. At this point, the purge is nothing more than a power-hungry grab for control of the overarching governing body."

I stared at Colt dumbfounded. My first thought was why hadn't I ever heard of blood substitutes before, and second was why hadn't I known there were vampires out there that opposed the purge. A governor's son, nonetheless.

I opened my mouth to say something, but I was cut off by a knock at the door.

"Come in," Colt called.

"Wait no! What-" I stared mortified as the door cracked open, and Finn walked inside.

I shielded my face and sank down as far as I could in the tub.

"I'm sorry, brother, I didn't know that you had company." The twin smiled at me with a maniacal grin. He held a drink in his hand, obviously oblivious to the fact that it was six in the morning. "Found another plaything, did you?"

"What do you want, Finn?" Colt sounded even less enthused than before.

"I just came to see if you were awake. Father wants you to meet with the governor from triad one today about your takeover, and I wanted to see if you were ready."

"I'll be there. Now get out." Colt nudged Finn out of the room and closed the door.

"Oh thank god," I sighed, finally sitting up straight.

Out of nowhere, Finn appeared in the room again, and I screamed. I couldn't help it. I was tired, I was jumpy, and over all on edge.

"I'm guessing teleportation is his power?" I groaned.

All it took was a single look from Colt to send Finn teleporting out of the room.

"What takeover was he talking about?" I asked.

"It doesn't matter," Colt said quickly. "You can sleep in here if you want. I'm about to leave anyway." He slowly pulled his pants down to his ankles and pulled his shirt over his head exposing his finely cut abs. I tried to look away, but I couldn't; it was like a train wreck.

A very handsome train wreck.

"What? Do vampires have no sense of privacy?"

"More like no sense of shame." He flashed his white fangs and pushed back his tousled hair after slipping into a slick black suit.

I wanted to protest sleeping in his room, but I knew that he probably already knew what I was going to say.

And I didn't have any clean clothes. I wasn't about to do the walk of shame from his room to mine, even if it was good for my *image*. I'd wait until he was gone, nap for a bit, then sneak into my room.

Plus, if I was missing from my room, everyone would probably figure I was sleeping late after a hookup anyway. Same effect as the walk of shame idea, except I didn't have to let everyone see me naked. And anything that spared me even a single shred of decency was worth it.

Colt tossed me the T-shirt he'd been wearing to wear to nap.

"Exactly. I'll be your fake hookup, and you can be mine," Colt read my mind. "I could have my uses for a fake love interest. It could be fun." With that, he closed the door behind him and left me alone in a lukewarm bath with my thoughts as my only companion.

CHAPTER 11

I woke up to Veda shaking me violently.

"Scarlett, thank god I found you!"

My eyes slowly crept open, and for a split second, I felt the sheer panic of sleep amnesia: the first few seconds of waking up that rob you of your memories and leave you wondering where you are and what year it is.

"Scarlett. You need to get up now!"

I sat up and rubbed at my eyes. Bright ways of sunshine flooded in from the windows, nearly blinding me.

"What time is it?" I mumbled after my mind finally caught back up to reality.

I was stuck in the elusive stage between sleep and consciousness, the sticky one that didn't ever want to let anyone go.

"It's a little after ten." Veda's words were hurried. "You missed the press conference." *Crap.* My eyes finally opened, and they were wide with fear. The press conference was the nationally televised briefing that the government held to keep New York a watched city. Sure, the trials were advertised and aired nationwide, but the only people who were truly invested were the people of New York City. To everyone else it was just a sport; to New York, it meant the difference of who got to live and who got to die.

"Shit hit the fan," Veda's eyes got wide.

The fear in her face gave me a bad feeling in the pit of my stomach.

"I don't have time to explain here. It's not safe. Vinny's waiting for you in your room, you need to get there. Now." She didn't even wait for my response before she grabbed me by the arm and ripped me to my feet. My mind was reeling as she dragged me down the hall toward my suite. Around us people scattered about, left and right.

It definitely wasn't this busy yesterday. What the hell is going on?

We turned the corner and heard the Governor from Triad three approaching. Veda quickly pulled me into a supply closet and covered my mouth.

"Where the hell is the little bitch?" The Governor seethed. "Do you know how hard it is to lose the only female contender? I told you guys to keep an eye on her. It was your only job!" he screamed.

"Yes, sir. We're on it," Two of his security officers said in unison before all three stormed off further down the hall.

"Veda, what is happening?" My eyes were wide.

She pulled me from the closet, and we quickly moved toward my suite.

Veda went into the suite first to make sure it was safe. The room was ransacked; clothes were scattered all over the floor. Veda motioned for me to come inside and closed the door tightly behind us, sliding the lock into place.

"Veda, what-" My words were cut short by a faint cough coming from the other side of the bed. Veda and I exchanged looks and cautiously peered to the other side.

"Oh my god, Vinny!" My eyes filled with tears.

Vinny lay on the floor in a pool of blood. One of his eyes was swollen completely shut, his lip was busted, and the other one was turning black quick. His leg was bent in an unnatural shape, and his breathing was rough. Blood poured out in spirts form a stab wound in his stomach.

Veda covered her mouth to hold in a scream.

"Vinny! No, no, no, no, no." Tears poured from her eyes, and she lost it. "No, baby. No. This wasn't how this was supposed to go."

I helped Veda pull him to a sitting position propped against the wall; he groaned the whole time.

"Somebody tell me what the hell is going on!"

Vinny pulled his face from between Veda's shaking hands and looked at me.

"It looks like you have more people rooting for you than just me, kid." he coughed, winded by the few words.

"The national human rights organization," Veda added. "They took a liking to you. They've already been outraged about the trials for decades, but you were the last straw. It got out that your father was a member of their organization years ago, and your mother's going through cancer. The media ate it up, and the NHA adopted you as the face of their cause. People outside of New York really oppose the trials- like, a lot. And now it's all coming to a head, because of you." A shaky, tear filled smile spread across Veda's face. "This might all come to an end, because of you."

"Imagine that. A world without the trials," Vinny coughed. "Terrance would have loved it," he smiled weakly at the thought of his son."

"Colt and Drax spoke up at the conference today. Protestors showed up from all across the country, vampire and human alike, and it pissed the governors off. But I've never seen them as mad as when their own sons said they opposed the trials too on live television, because of you."

My heart thudded loudly in my chest. "Why me? Why am I so god damn special in everyone's eyes?"

"Listen, kid, we don't have much time." Vinny's eye was half closed now. "They're moving the trials up to today. To this very minute. They want to throw you in that hell hole panicked and unprepared, but you're not. You hear me? You're smart, and you're charming, and you're the only woman. Don't let those things go to waste; use them."

I stared at Vinny blankly. Veda still sobbed at his side, and I couldn't help but picture my own father in his place, remembering the day that I found him slumped over in the alleyway behind the apartment buildings. He had the same look on his face, contentment. I'd always wondered how he could look so at peace with death breathing so closely down his neck, but I saw it in Vinny too.

My father's last words came to mind; they bounced around in my head.

Live your life, Scarlett. I'll be rooting for you.

I didn't understand his last words then. I didn't want to live my life, and for the next five years, I spent my time walking through life barely wanting to live at all. But now when death was knocking at my door begging to be let in, I'd made my choice.

I did want to live. If not for him or for my mother, for myself. And for Vinny and Veda, and all the other innocent people whose lives were turned to shit because of the toxic game that the governors played with human souls. The NHRA was right to protest it; the humans were right to protest it, and the vampires were right to protest it.

If we were ever going to be able to live in a world where vampires and humans could live in balance with one another, the

101

trials had to end.

And I was going to be the one to end them.

Vinny noticed the shift in my eyes, even on his death bed and forced another smile. He winced at the pain, but I could tell it was worth it. "You got this. We're all rooting for the underdog, okay? Go with the sword. You look badass with a sword." He coughed and used the rest of his strength to point to the outfit we'd chosen for the trials. "The plan's still on. You're just a pretty face until they get close enough for a kill, you hear me?"

I nodded. By then, the tears that were dancing on the edges of my eyes were spilling over to my cheeks, but I didn't care anymore.

"It was a pleasure training you, Scarlett, even for a day. Now go."

Veda handed me my outfit and a cloak to wear over it. I rushed to the bathroom to change and tied the cloak around my neck. Veda ushered me out of the doorway and into the hallway.

"Are you coming with me?" I asked. My heart was racing too fast for me to even realize how panicked I felt. I was a ball of pure adrenaline.

"He's the love of my life. I can't let him die alone." Veda forced a smile. "Go. Win for us. Take those bastards down."

I nodded. I knew she didn't mean the contenders; she meant the governors. Their days were numbered, and they knew it.

Veda sent me off with a hug. I pulled the hood of my red velvet cloak over my head and scurried down the hall toward the training room. The hallways were clear now and eerily quiet. There were no contenders rushing around, no security officers, and no governors. Not a single soul but my own, and it didn't sit right on my nerves.

I made my way to the training room, slipped inside, and breathed a sigh of relief that it was empty. The weapons were all still there.

I pulled the gorgeous sword from the wall and strapped a sheath to my waist. I holstered a gun to my hip and slid some extra bullets into the pockets sewn inside of my cloak. I turned to leave, and Finn teleported through the door and stood directly in front of me.

My eyes widened.

"There you are. You have a hell of a lot of people looking for you. Angry people." He scowled.

"I'm guessing you're one of them." I glared. My hand rested on the handle of the sword.

"I don't know what kind of radical ideas you planted inside of Colt's weak head, and I'm surprised that an addict like Drax was even sober enough for you to influence, but you did it somehow. You single handedly found a way to fuck up a lifetime of work and even more possibilities for them *and* me. For what? Why you? What makes you so special?"

I wondered the same, but I refused to let him see me falter. Vinny wasn't going to die for nothing. I refused to let him die in vain like my father.

"Because I'm the one that's going to bring this whole thing down," I said the words, but they didn't feel real coming out of my mouth. I wanted to believe them, but there was a part inside of me that couldn't. I was still working on filling the shoes I was forced to put on.

Finn was beyond angry; he was pissed off beyond the point of return. He definitely didn't see whatever Drax and Colt did. He took a step forward, and I was seconds away from pulling the sword from my side. I barely knew how to work it, but there wasn't a better time than the present to learn.

The door to the training room swung open, and a hoard of security agents flooded in. They had on full swat gear and aimed high powered rifles directly at my head.

Nothing like bringing a sword to a gun fight.

I let go of the handle and held both of my hands up in the air. I wasn't about to get shot point blank before the trials even started. I couldn't win the trials if I wasn't alive.

"We got 'em, boss. En route now," one spoke into the radio that was fastened to his shoulder.

"Wait? What the hell do you mean them?" Finn snarled. "I'm not with-" His words were cut off when a tranquilizer dart shot out of one of the rifles. He teleported to the corner of the room and the dart hit the wall. "What the hell!" Finn screamed from across the room.

The agents panicked, and they all started firing their tranq guns at once; the sounds of the shots vibrated off the solid walls and assaulted my ear drums. I looked down to see three darts sunken deep into my thigh. I looked up at Finn as he tried to fight the agents in hand to hand combat.

"I'm not with her, you idiots!" he yelled.

"Our orders come straight from the governors themselves," one said through his helmet.

The edges of my vision frayed, and the last thing I remembered was seeing five agents hold him down while three tranquilized him at the same time.

CHAPTER 12

My hearing was the first of my senses to come back. Someone rustled and rifled through a stack of papers somewhere close. Then my sense of smell slowly resurfaced, and the air smelled stagnant and old, like it was coated with a thick layer of dust. Next, I felt the cold, hard floor beneath me, pushing against my body. I fought hard to force my body to move, but my muscles denied my every order. It was the most terrifying feeling I'd ever experienced, being paralyzed. Thankfully, it only lasted for a few minutes before my finger finally twitched, then I was able to make a fist, and my eyes finally opened. I shot straight up, gasping for air and clutching my chest.

My chest heaved, and every inch of my body was sore, especially my thigh, where three red dots remained from the darts that had been lodged into it.

I was in an old hotel room, one that no one had been in for years, by the look of it. A thick layer of dust covered nearly everything, and by the burn in my lungs, I guessed that an even thicker cloud of it hung in the air and coated my lungs.

Drax and Finn still lay tranquilized on the two king sized beds, and Colt stood in front of the old desk in the corner, flipping through various pieces of paper.

"Where are we?" I coughed and waived a cloud of dust from my face.

"The outskirts. The playground for the trials this year, I guess." Colt didn't pull his eyes from whatever he was examining.

"The outskirts?" My heart raced. The outskirts were what remained of the city after the takeover. They built a set of giant walls around what parts of the city were salvageable and declared the rest the outskirts, a dumping ground for waste, chemicals, and deplorables. I'd thought it was only a myth, a fairytale that they told children to keep them from growing into adults with a sense of adventure. I didn't know that it was real.

"Wait, wait, wait. If this is the trials, why are you here?" Everything about this was confusing. "What happened?"

Colt turned to me. There was a look in his eyes that I couldn't quite pin. It was a mix of anger and determination, with a splash of vengeance thrown in.

He set down the papers and offered me a hand to help me stand.

"I met a naked girl in my room at six in the morning who wasn't afraid to tell me how it is," he smirked. "It might have seemed small and awkward to you, but it was big for me. It opened up my eyes to how truly fucked the world we live in is, and how truly blessed I was to be in a position of power. So I used that power."

"To fuck shit up," I smiled.

"Yes, that's one way to put it," he smiled. "I saw an opportunity on live television to take a match to the gasoline of change that's been seeping into our entire country for years. You aren't the only one who noticed the disparity and wanted change."

Behind us, Finn groaned, trying to sit up. "And you bastards just had to drag me in to your quest for equality." He nursed a dried cut on his forehead.

"Guilty by association, I'm afraid," Colt half laughed.

I hadn't noticed before, but Finn didn't share Colt's accent.

"That would also be attributed to my years of being raised by nannies," Colt answered my question before I could even ask it. "I was raised away from here, far off in a country where things are done a lot differently than this shit show."

"If it's a shit show then why did you come back?" Finn snapped. He sat on the edge of the bed now, and I watched as the life slowly came back to him. With the life came the anger that I had gotten just a glimpse of before.

"We both know father summoned me for the transition. And when father calls, you have no choice but to answer."

What the hell is that? I turned to look at Colt.

"Five years ago, the governor of triad one's son was killed during the purge. Contrary to popular belief, vampires are not immortal; all it takes is a decapitation to take us out forever. A group of radicals offed him in triad three, leaving triad one short an heir for the governor throne."

Triad three, that's mine. I thought back to that night. I hadn't even known that a governor's son died that night; they must have been keeping it as quiet as they could.

"My father set up a deal for me to assume the place as heir. After all, he had an extra son lying around off in England that he wasn't making use of, so why not put him to work, right?" Colt rolled his eyes. "None of this made sense to me at all, not for the longest time. I didn't know why they decided to make an amendment to add women to the trials, I didn't know why they wanted to change everything this year. To be quite honest, I had just been grateful up until then to be as far away from the sadistic city as I was. That was until I read the governor's minds and saw the memories of the man who killed the *prince* of triad one," Colt mocked.

"What the hell does that have to do with me, or anything for that matter?"

"I told you, your insides were interesting," Colt blushed, realizing what he'd said. "Your mind, anyway. I searched and searched your mind until I came across your father. Your father was the man responsible for the killing; he was defending your apartment from the entitled prick. It was no accident that you were the first and only girl picked for the trials. The daughter of the human rights agent who killed a governor's son. They're making an example of you, so I had no choice but to make an example of them.

I stumbled backward and braced myself against the bed. My mind was reeling, and I felt like I was going to be sick. This entire thing, the elaborate summoning, the mind games, the man hunt. It was all for me. All for some governor's sick need for validation and revenge?

Thousands of men and women were going to die, and it was kind of my fault.

"This is all suspenseful and inspirational and fantastic, but if you guys don't mind me, I'm going to make my way out of this shit hole and explain to our dad that I had nothing to do with this little threesome of mutiny or whatever it is that you guys have going on here." Finn got up from the bed.

"You think just because you kiss his ass, you're safe?" Colt called.

His words stopped Finn at the door.

"I've read his mind, Finn. He doesn't give a shit about anyone. That includes you."

Finn clenched his fists tightly and stood frozen in the doorway. On the bed beside me, Drax had finally woken up, but he knew not to say a word. We both had the feeling that we were about to witness an actual murder right in front of our eyes. The first kill of the trials was about to go down right in our dingy little hiding spot.

Finn teleported directly in front of Colt; their faces were only inches apart.

"You don't get to judge me," he snapped. "You don't get to say a damn thing about how I act or what I do. You had a way out. A ticket to freedom with a shiny English life. You left me!" Finn's voice cracked, and so did his emotional walls. "You left me in this hell hole. It was just me and my fucking anger for years, simmering in this garbage fire. I did what I had to do to survive, to make him love me," he paused, and his words hung in the air like a cloud of dust. "And it still wasn't enough," he muttered quietly before erupting in tears. Colt opened his arms and embraced his brother.

Drax and I raised a brow at each other. We didn't need to say a word; both of our expressions screamed, *What the fuck is going on?!* The vibe went from witnessing a murder to watching a tender episode of your favorite soap opera in about thirty seconds. I had to admit, it was nice seeing Finn wasn't a complete monster either. Maybe there were other vampires like him out there, forced to be the monsters that everyone else already labeled them to be just to be accepted by their own kind.

Nobody was really what they seemed, and it was all the more reason for me to make it out of this game alive and bring an end to the trials. Hell, I was ready to bring an end to the entire government and anybody who ever condoned separation by species again.

I was ready to give cohabitation with vampires a chance, but I had to survive first.

Somewhere outside, the loud siren sounded, alerting all players that the trials were officially beginning.

The low hum of a motor was approaching.

"Do you guys hear that?"

"The drones. Everybody get down!" Finn yelled.

We all hit the floor. Drax and I cowered behind the bed, and Colt and Finn jumped into the closet. A flying drone slowly approached the window and stopped outside. It was so close, I could hear the hum of the propellers. It hovered outside the window for a minute before deciding that we must have left and made its way elsewhere.

I looked down to realize I was laying directly on Drax. He had a perverted smile on his face.

"All it took was facing our deaths to get you close to me? I would have done this yesterday if I knew." He winked.

I rolled my eyes and got to my feet.

"They're still televising this? Even with everything going on?"

"Any publicity is good publicity," Finn mumbled. "The wise words of dear old dad."

He wiped a stream of tears from his face, and he was looking more and more like himself.

"So what do we do now? How the hell do we stop this? Or win it? Or whatever our plan is," I asked. I had no idea what was even happening anymore.

"Well, they're desperate. When you're desperate, you get sloppy, and them throwing all of us in the trials was as sloppy as it could possibly get."

"Why?"

"We've got information that most contenders don't. We know the trials inside and out, and that means we know how to flip the switch on this entire thing."

Finn nodded, which was reassuring. As much as he probably hated me, and as much as he acted like a dick, it was true that he probably had the most information to win than any of us.

We all turned to him for our next move.

He paced the room for a second and thought.

"Well, Scarlett is the face of this movement, right? The human rights people chose her and her story to light the flames that are threatening to burn the entire system down. All we need to do is get her in front of the world. All it'll take is one sentence from her to tell everyone to burn the city to the ground. There are millions of humans in the country; we've done the math, and they actually outnumber us. That was one of the reasons for the trials, to keep them from banding together. If we could get her in front of them and give them enough hope, they just might dismantle this thing from the inside. We won't even have to set foot inside of the city. "

"And they already did the hard work for us televising the event, right? All we have to do is find the right equipment, hijack their signal and uplink ourselves to their network. With the right algorithm and man power, we could easily takeover their broadcast," Drax added.

We all turned and stared at him in awe.

"What? I'm actually good at doing some things you know," he said. "Besides drugs," he mumbled at the end.

"Are you up for it, Scarlett?" Colt asked.

I thought for a minute. I was already there, forced to live through the hell of the trials. If I had a chance to make the governors feel even an ounce of the pain that they'd caused over the years, it was worth any risk.

"I'm in." I smiled.

CHAPTER 13

We all crowded around the rickety desk in the corner. We had to squeeze in tight for everyone to see, and I was in the middle. I would have been lying if I said my body being pressed in between all of them didn't give me a rush, but I might have been hopped up on adrenaline too.

The closer I looked, the more I got a feel for why Colt was ravaging through the papers; they were maps. The desk was covered in different types of maps. It looked like he had gotten as much information about the outskirts as he could, printed them off and crumpled them up in his jacket pocket before they tranquilized him.

"That's exactly what I did," Colt answered. "I knew this year they were trying to surprise the contenders with a new setting, and they thought no one knew that it would take place in the outskirts. But I pride myself on keeping my ability a secret for this very reason. I grabbed as much intel as I could before they took me down."

"You smart bastard," Drax smiled. He leaned in closer to the map and squinted. "So if I'm not mistaken, the famous opera house is on the corner of Fifth Street and Whey Avenue. It was one of the first set up in the city that had television broadcasting capabilities. The tech is probably outdated, but I'm sure I could fix it up good enough to hijack their broadcast."

We all stared at Drax again; it was weird hearing things come out of his mouth that didn't involve whiskey or women. He had layers, ones that nobody else knew about, and it was kind of refreshing. The more I got to know him, the more I realized that he was like me, more than just a pretty face.

"There it is," Colt put his finger down on the map. "Now we just have to figure out where the bloody hell we are, and we've got ourselves a plan."

I glanced around the room. This was a hotel; there had to be something in here that had the address. "Here!" I picked up a to go menu that was covered in dust. It had the hotel address on the front.

"Oh, I could kiss you right now," Colt sighed. "I mean if we weren't trying to survive. You know, maybe under different circumstances. Not that there's anything wrong with the circumstances, it's just-"

"Colt," I shushed. "The map."

"Right, yes." He searched the map and found the hotel. "We're exactly on the opposite end of the city. It's at least a two day walk to get there, and that's if the other contenders don't off us before that."

"Or the radioactive weather storms," Drax nodded.

My eyes widened. "What the hell kind of stuff were they dumping out here?"

There was a loud crash in the hallway, and all of our heads snapped in that direction.

"Guys, what do you think the odds are that we're the only contenders that were dropped at this hotel?" My heart raced. I knew I'd have to fight, and possibly kill, to get through the trials, but I didn't think that it was going to happen right away. I needed time to ease myself into the chaos.

"Slim. Even the agents don't want to be out in this territory. It's no-man's land, and anything goes. There's no telling what kind of creatures have been breeding outside the city walls. They would have dropped multiple contestants at multiple landing spots to minimize their own exposure." Finn really did know his way around the trials, and his father's government for that matter. I could definitely see him sitting in the governor throne ordering people around.

"We better get out of here, fast." Colt grabbed the map and stuffed it into his coat.

"Scarlett, you're the one with all the weapons so you have to go first."

"What? No! I don't think this is what they meant when they

invented the ladies first rule!" I protested.

Finn nudged me forward. He was right; there was no time to argue. Every second that passed was another second that whoever, or whatever, was out there could get the jump on us.

I took a deep breath and thought of Vinny, and Veda, and my mom. They were the people I was doing this for, and I had to be brave. The trials were no place for the weak.

I pulled my handgun from my thigh, relieved that the agents had been too stupid to pat me down, and slowly opened the door. I winced at the loud squeaking noise that cut through the thick layer of dust-covered silence and held my breath. I prayed that whatever was out there had already made its way to a different floor and tucked itself away in a different room. Maybe it was as afraid of us as we were of it.

I slowly peeked my head out of the doorway and out into the hallway. My eyes locked on to a large golden treasure chest that shimmered in the dim light. It sat at the end of the hall with its lid wide open.

That must be one of the supplies chests that they scatter around the arena.

My heart sank at the fact that it was open. There was no way a wild dog or a bear would be able to raid a supplies chest; that meant one thing. There was at least one other contender in the building with us. Probably in the hall.

But my curiosity got to me. I needed to see what was inside.

Maybe they left something behind that we can put to use.

"Be careful." Colt whispered after obviously overhearing my thoughts. I nodded and inched out into the hallway barrel first, one step at a time. Every few steps I took, a plume of dust would puff up from the horrid red carpet, and I'd have to shield my eyes.

So far so good.

I'd made it half way down the hallway far easier than I'd anticipated. I took another step, and a floorboard creaked underneath my foot.

There was a loud bang as a gun went off from somewhere down the hall, and the shot connected with the wall beside me. I quickly jumped into an open doorway and used it for cover. I waited until the smoke cleared and peaked my head out again.

Nothing.

Whoever it was, they were good at hiding but a horrible shot. I thanked god that my father had brought me to the shooting range when I was a kid. It was our bonding time. He was the type of person that believed that everyone should know how to shoot, especially in the times that we lived in. If you didn't have fangs, you were already at a disadvantage; a gun was the next best thing.

An old dictionary lay on the floor beside me. I picked it up and tossed it into the hallway. A head popped out of the doorway, and they fired a shot without thinking.

Gotcha.

I squeezed my trigger, and my bullet struck him in the shoulder.

There was a piercing cry, and I saw his gun skid across the hallway. I saw my chance, and I took it. I charged at him with my gun still drawn. It was a guy, not much older than me by the looks of it. He had chocolate brown hair and deep blue eyes. The scruff on his chin told me that he hadn't shaved in a while.

"Give me one reason why I shouldn't kill you right now," I said with the barrel pointed in his face.

He clutched his shoulder, but it wasn't enough to keep the blood from spilling out.

"We're from the same triad. You're the chick, right? The only one summoned."

"Obviously," I muttered. "Why is that a reason I shouldn't shoot you in the face right now?"

"Because we're on the same team. We both want the same thing, our triad to win."

I sighed and lowered my weapon. "You want our triad to win, I want to shut this shit down. We *don't* want the same thing." I motioned for the guys to come out, and they followed close behind. The chest was still full of supplies; he must have just had enough time to pull a single weapon from it before he realized he wasn't alone and took cover.

"You really think that you can do that? Bring an end to all of this?" he asked.

I pulled the medic supplies from the chest and knelt next to him. I pulled his hand from his wound, packed it, and wrapped it tightly. He winced at the pressure.

"This thing has been holding humans down for generations. You'll never get out. None of us ever will."

"Not with that attitude we won't," I said. I got to my feet and offered him a hand up. "Come with us."

The three guys stared at me blankly. They didn't have to say a word. I knew they thought I was crazy to offer to help him, especially in a to-the-death match of survival. But if I let the trials take whatever humanity that I had left, they won. Everyone who ever supported the games would get what they wanted, and I'd let Vinny and Veda and everyone else who was counting on me down.

The guy looked confused at first, but he nodded. I drew my weapon and led us through the halls, down the staircase, and into a grand lobby. The ceilings were so high they reminded me of an old school cathedral, and it had the architecture to match. My feet clacked loudly against the marble floor. I couldn't help but wonder what life was like before the vampire takeover. A piece of me yearned to live in a world where people stayed in places like that for fun. Anything beat the shit show era that I lived in.

"You know, it was really nice of you to bring me with. My name's Bobby," he said.

"Nice to meet you, Bobby," I mumbled, trying to focus on the task at hand. We slowly crept through the revolving door with busted glass panels and shuffled out onto the street.

"No really, I really appreciate it," Bobby continued. "It was ballsy, and I love a woman with balls as much as the next guy, so I'm going to clue you in on a little secret that I don't think you know."

"I'm listening," I raised a brow.

"You see, the governors changed the rules last minute, right before they dropped us in the game. Switched up the teams a little bit."

"The teams? To what?"

I couldn't figure out a scenario that would make sense. I doubted that they'd pair people from different triads together because then they'd have to spare two from the purge instead of just one.

"They changed the motive. Offered a butt load of cash and freedom to the winning team," he smiled.

"And what are the teams?"

"Us against you." Before I could process what was happening, he pulled a gun out from underneath his shirt and aimed it directly at me. I froze. My brain couldn't work fast enough, and he pulled the trigger.

I closed my eyes, and it felt like time slowed. In a split second, my brain pulled me through my entire lifetime and the things I'd done. I realized I never really got a chance to be myself and to get to know who I was as a person because I went from being a kid straight to the caretaker of a widowed cancer patient. It stung, but I knew I'd do it all over again if I was given the chance.

The thundering boom came from the gun, but before the bullet could reach me, Finn jumped in front of me. The bullet cut into his side, and he dropped to the ground.

"They're over here!" Bobby screamed as loudly as he could. "They're over-" his scream was cut off by a sharp dagger to the throat. His knees buckled underneath him, and Drax stood behind him holding the knife awkwardly.

"Remember when I said I wasn't a killer?" Drax tossed the blade on the ground next to him. "Ugh, and this was my favorite suit. Now look at it!" he whined.

Somewhere off in the distance, a shot went off. Finn groaned on the ground.

"Quick, help me get him up. We need to take cover, and we need to do it fast."

Colt helped me sling one of Finn's arms over my shoulder, and we made our way down the street.

CHAPTER 14

"How long were we tranquilized for?" I asked as we dragged Finn down the street in the fading daylight. It was only ten in the morning when I went down, but the abandoned city was already bathing in the golden orange light of sunset.

Finn was bleeding, and he was bleeding bad. I didn't know that vampires could even bleed, but I guess there were a lot of things that I didn't know about vampires.

There was an explosion behind us. We all turned to see a huge plume of smoke erupt from the direction of the Hotel, followed by a thundering noise.

The building was going down.

"They bombed the entire fucking thing!" Drax yelled out. There was a hint of excitement in his voice. He was feeding off the chaotic energy. He was probably used to almost dying; the parties he went to were insane. People probably nearly died at them every day.

"Here is a good place," I nodded towards an abandoned corner store. It reminded me of the kind that sold groceries and every type of cigarette known to man. It had a lot of windows, which wasn't the best for hiding from people who were trying to slaughter you, but as the sun dipped down past the horizon, I knew it was the best choice that we had.

Drax pulled the door open that was surprisingly unlocked, and we carted Finn inside. He groaned, but by then, he was already sliding in and out of consciousness. Drax stood as lookout by the front door, and Colt and I pulled him into a small room in the back. It looked like it had been an old employee's lounge. It had a single table, a few chairs, and a broken-down vending machine.

We pulled him up onto the table, and I lifted up his shirt. His toned abs were streaked with smears of red.

"Why the hell isn't he regenerating? Don't you guys regenerate?" I asked panicked at the amount of blood that was spurting out of the hole in his side.

"We do, unless we're weak, or we haven't fed in a while." His eyes met mine. "Or the bullet's laced with tarragon."

He read my mind.

I knew what I had to do. "Hand me the medic bag." I rummaged through and found a pair of tweezers.

"Finn, this is going to hurt like hell; please don't kill me." I had never said that phrase and meant it as literally as I did in that moment as I plunged the tweezers into his wound. Colt rushed to his side and held him down as he writhed.

"Guys! Someone's coming, make him be quiet!" Drax panicked as he peered out the window.

Colt rolled up an extra t shirt that he grabbed from the chest and shoved it in Finn's mouth to muffle his screams.

"He's going to kill me after this." Colt whispered.

"Let's hope I get this bullet out before the tarragon hits his blood system so he can live long enough to kill us." I shoved the tweezers deeper, and Finn shook.

"I have it! I got it!" I pulled the small bullet out and held it in front of me as proof.

"Everyone quiet," Drax whispered.

Finn breathed heavily on the table, but his muscles relaxed. I wasn't the only one that was relieved the bullet was finally out.

Colt and I left Finn in the back and quietly moved out into the main store area with Drax. Through the dirty glass, I saw a group of three men slowly walking down the street. One carried a chainsaw, the other held a rifle, and the last had a large automatic.

They eyed every building suspiciously, but I could tell by the frustration on their faces that they had no idea where we were. I pulled my sword from its sheath just in case. I was done underestimating people and trusting them too much. If I learned anything from

Bobby's betrayal, it was that humanity and stupidity were two different things. Finn was on the table bleeding out because of my stupidity, and I wasn't about to let that happen to anyone else.

The sunlight was fading and with every minute, the men looked less like men and more like shadow figures. They stopped directly in the middle of the street, and we all ducked underneath the window. We held our breath and prayed that they didn't see us.

A thundering boom sounded and vibrated the entire building.

What the hell?

I peeked out the window just in time to see one of them pull the pin on what looked like a grenade and toss it into a random building.

They're throwing at random, trying to flush us out.

Colt nodded his head quietly and signaled for Drax not to panic. After a few minutes of silence, the men gave up and continued down the street. I felt like I could finally breathe again.

I made my way back to the back room and yelled for Colt.

Finn lay motionless on the table. A look of terror spread over Colt's face, and he rushed to do CPR.

"I thought you guys were immortal! How is this even happening?" My eyes started to water.

"We don't have time for your outdated ideologies of vampires, Scarlett! I need help!" Colt snapped.

I had never heard him raise his voice like that. It sounded weird coming out of such a mellow person; that's how I knew Finn was in some deep shit.

"He needs blood, otherwise he can't heal himself, Scarlett, and you're the only one with human blood coursing through their veins."

I didn't hesitate. I took my sword from its sheath and poked it into the center of my hand. It burned, and I was impressed with how sharp the blade was. I winced at the pain, and a pool of thick red blood started to fill my palm.

Colt moved out of the way, and I brought my hand to Finn's mouth and let some of the blood drop into it. I held my breath and prayed that he'd wake up. I'd never forgive myself if he died protecting me, especially right at the start of the trials. It would be a waste of his life.

"Nothing's happening; why is nothing happening?" I panicked.

Colt let out a sigh. "There's no way to tell until he wakes up. Just keep giving him steady streams of it, okay?" With that, Colt turned and left the small breakroom to get some air.

For the next ten minutes, I slowly gave Finn doses of my blood until I started to feel dizzy and had to sit down. I wrapped my hand tightly to stop the bleeding and sighed.

I went over the situation in my head again and again. I was stupid. I was careless, and I was naive. Even a blind person would have known not to trust Bobby. Not only was it a rookie mistake, but it was a rookie mistake that might take Finn's life.

I wallowed for a few minutes before Colt came back into the room and slumped down beside me. I looked in his eyes, and for the first time since I'd met him, he was on edge. Drax was always on edge and fidgety; Finn was always uptight, but Colt? He was the mellow one.

"I'm sorry. This is all my fault," I mumbled.

Colt clenched his jaw. I didn't have to read minds to know that he was debating on which road to take: the low road or the high one. Finn was an asshat, but he meant a lot to Colt; it was obvious.

"He was right about me abandoning him," Colt said quietly.

"I know that's not true. You said you were just a kid when your father sent you away."

"Yes, but he gave me the option to stay. And I didn't. Finn doesn't know, but it's something that's haunted me every day since. I really meant to come back one day, but I couldn't. I just felt so fucking ashamed of myself. I knew how our father was. I knew what I was leaving him behind in, and I left anyway."

Colt looked up at me with tears in his eyes. He loved his brother, that was obvious, even by the way he was there to hold Finn up when he broke down. Deep in his eyes, there was a sadness that he tried to hide behind books and facts and knowledge. But he couldn't do that anymore, so there he sat with his soul on display for me, and I realized then that vampires do have souls. They have pain, and they have feelings, and they can die just like humans.

What I did next was completely out of character for me. Under normal circumstances, I wouldn't go around pulling people in for hugs, but I felt like normal flew out the window ages ago. We were fighting for survival now. We'd started our friendship off naked, so what was a hug, right? I pulled him in and squeezed him tightly. His cologne smelled warm and sweet. He held me back tightly, and a surge of warmth grew in my chest. For once, I wasn't worried if he could read my thoughts because my mind was blank. I was completely in the moment, moving off of instinct. He pulled away, and before I realized what was happening, he pulled me in for a kiss. His warm, soft lips pressed against mine, and a surge of electricity sparked below my waist. When the initial shock passed, I kissed him back. What started out as something innocent blossomed into a wildfire of passion within seconds. His hand traveled up my back and cradled my face. I glided my fingertips over his tight chest and interlocked them behind his neck.

Colt pulled away, and the look in his eyes changed. "You truly are an enigma, Scarlett Johnson. Any man would be lucky to even grace your presence."

Our eyes lingered on one another for a few more seconds before Colt smiled and got to his feet. He left the room for a minute before returning with a small blanket and a travel sized pillow. He laid it on the ground beside me.

"You sleep in here with Finn, and Drax and I will keep watch. Okay?"

The mere mention of the word sleep made me realize how drowsy I really was.

"Are you sure you guys will be okay?"

"Yeah, we'll rotate sleeping out there. It's hard for me to see him like this." Colt clenched his jaw tightly.

I nodded. I understood. I barely knew Finn, and it was hard for me to see him like that. But I was the one who got us all into this mess, so I was going to be the one to sit by his side until he woke up or he died. My stomach churned at the thought, and I hoped Colt didn't pick up on my lack of faith in the situation.

He smiled slightly before going out into the main area to relieve Drax.

I sat with my thoughts, which arguably made the worst company ever. My mind wandered to the national human rights organization. I hated that the world I lived in had me conditioned to wonder if anyone could be trusted, even an organization that was dedicated to fighting for my rights. But I couldn't help but wonder why they decided to speak up about the trials now; why not start an uproar when the men were getting killed? Was I really able to be the one to unite the world against the atrocity?

I'm definitely not going to be of any use to anyone if I don't get any sleep. I rubbed at my eyes with a balled fist.

Fighting for my life was surprisingly exhausting and not just physically. I laid my head down and slid into the welcoming darkness.

CHAPTER 15

E ven my sleep was tortured by the threat of the games. I tossed and turned, but even in my dreams, I couldn't escape them.

I sat up, gasping for air, clutching my throat.

"It's about time you woke up. I was starting to think that you were the one that was dead." I looked up to see Finn sitting upright on the table.

I breathed a sigh of relief. "Finn, oh thank god you're okay!" I jumped to my feet and hugged him.

I guess the trials were making me a hugger. Who would have

guessed?

"We have to tell Colt. He's going to be so stoked." I turned to go grab him, but Finn grabbed my wrist and held me back.

"No don't. I already went out there to check on him, and he was asleep. Drax said he held out for as long as he could, but he finally let him take over as lookout and decided to get some sleep. He needs to sleep."

He was right. Colt probably stayed awake worrying himself to death.

"So how are you feeling? That bullet was laced with tarragon."

"I know. I can feel it." He twisted a little and winced.

"I just want to say thank you for jumping in front of that bullet for me. I froze. If it weren't for you, I wouldn't have come back from it as easy." I looked around the room, awkwardly avoiding eye contact.

The truth was, I didn't really even know why I couldn't look him in the yes. He just jumped in front of a bullet for me, and I couldn't even repay him with eye contact.

"Thanks, by the way," he mumbled. "For the blood. I wouldn't have made it out if it weren't for that."

I nodded. With Colt, it was easy to talk. He was chill, laid back. Hell, even Drax was easier to talk to thank Finn was. Finn was intimidating and brutishly charming. All things that I wouldn't have thought I'd find myself attracted to in a million years, but standing there, I finally let myself admit that I was.

"So, how did that gun hurt you? I thought vampires were

immortal, or invincible, or whatever." I felt stupid even asking.

Finn smirked. 'You've been watching too many movies, but that's exactly what our dads want people to think. The truth is vampires can be killed if it involves tarragon. We live really long, but we're not immortal. Super sexy and handsome? Yes. Immortal? No."

I sat for a minute, mulling over my thoughts. It felt like every day the guys found a way to make me realize that everything I thought I knew about vampires was a load of shit. I thought about how many humans in the city still cowered under vampire control, believing the ruse that they were all powerful and all knowing.

If the entire city knew what I knew, would things be different?

"So, we should talk," Finn cleared his throat. He sounded determined.

I blushed, hoping he didn't secretly have the power to read minds too?

"Yeah?" I tried not to stutter.

"I don't think putting us in the trials was a last-minute decision."

My eyes widened.

Colt appeared in the doorway. "Because there's no way they would have had time to add tarragon weapons to the map. The map was stocked weeks ago."

What he said bounced around in my head.

"But that would mean-"

"That they were planning on putting us in the trials weeks ago," Finn finished my sentence.

None of it made sense. I didn't understand.

I was about to fire off another question when a noise stopped me dead in my tracks- another siren. This one was different than the commencement one that let contenders know that it was time to start. It was the phase one siren. Before I could even register what was going on, the ground underneath my feet started to rumble. It started out as a low hum and turned to violent vibrations that shook the small building.

I froze and stared at Finn, wide eyed. Even he looked scared, and I knew that some deep shit was on its way.

"Phases? They're still doing phases? I thought they changed the rules!" I panicked.

"Unfortunately, they can change the rules however they want. There's no government entity overseeing the trials besides them. They can make it as sick and inhumane as they want."

"Guys! You have to come see this!" Drax yelled from the front of the store.

Finn hopped down from the table and dashed out front.

He must really be healed, I thought as I trailed behind him closely.

"What is it?" I peered out the dirty glass window. It was just after sunrise, and a heavy downpour drenched everything that the light touched.

I squinted in the direction that Drax was pointing. Far off in the distance, there was a huge wall of water tearing through the city, like a tsunami.

"We have to go, now!" Finn yelled. We burst out of the corner store, and we all ran as fast as we could. The ground beneath us rumbled and shook, and behind us, the water crashed loudly through the deserted city. It was so loud that I could barely hear my heart thundering in my chest.

Shots fired from an upper floor in one of the buildings that towered over us and pelted the street next to me as I ran. I ducked, frantically trying to find the shooter.

Another spray of bullets rained down on us. There was too much going on. I couldn't concentrate. I couldn't even imagine how the guys felt. Their senses were probably going insane.

Drax tossed me a gun that we'd snagged from the chest and another spray of bullets was unleashed on us. I heard the *tink* of one hitting a piece of my armor. It didn't go through, but the impact dented it and stung my skin good enough for me to wince.

I had to find where these bullets were coming from and fast. It was hard to focus over the incredible roar of the collateral damage of the wave.

I looked up, and for a split second, I saw a small flash of light, like a gun scope catching the sunrise just right.

Got you. I squeezed the trigger, and it soared through the air. A few second later, a body fell from the third story of a building up ahead and landed on the sidewalk below. I prayed that was the only one as we ran past it.

"We need to get to higher ground!" Drax screamed. His voice was nearly lost in the fray.

He was right. We couldn't outrun a flood surge like that; it was too big and coming way too fast. By the sounds of it, it was taking out all of the smaller, weaker buildings on its way to us.

Suddenly up ahead, I spotted another hotel; this one was much taller than the one we were dropped in. It towered about 20 stories into the sky.

I got the guys' attention and pointed to it, before I realized someone stood at the entryway, waving their arms frantically, trying to get our attention.

I picked my gun up and aimed directly at him. The closer we got, the more I could make out what the person looked like. It was a man in his early twenties like me. He had dark eyes and tanned skin that went well with the light brown scruff that covered his chin. His sandy hair matched.

I held my weapon steady as we made our way to him.

"Don't shoot, don't shoot. I need you to follow me." He held both his hands in the air.

Behind us, I could hear the water crashing closer and closer with every second.

"Tell me one reason why I shouldn't," I barked. I was done blindly trusting strangers. Bobby ruined it for me.

"Because I'm not part of the trials," he said.

I lowered my weapon for a second.

What? How is that even possible?

I raised it again, pointing it back at his strangely handsome face.

"And you really can't afford not to trust me at this point."

He nodded behind me, and I turned to see the rush of water come around the corner and flood onto the street, destroying everything in its path.

Point taken.

I lowered my gun, and he quickly ushered us inside. We made our way through the door and walked into a large and surprisingly clean hotel lobby. There wasn't a speck of dust on it, and the electricity even worked. The second we stepped inside, two large metal doors lid up from the floor and clamped tightly behind the flimsy glass ones we walked through. The same sheet of thick metal slid out from the windows and secured them too. The place was locked down, and it looked like it was airtight too, but I still wondered if his measures could hold up against a tidal wave of water like that.

Inside the lobby stood two guys with rifles, standing guard. The man nodded to them as we passed and quickly shuffled into an elevator on the opposite side. We piled in, and he hit the number twenty on the keypad. The elevator slowly lurched upward, and classical music started to play.

I looked at Colt, and he didn't even need to read my mind to know I was screaming *what the fuck* inside my head.

The elevator shot straight up, way faster than I was expecting, and my knees almost buckled underneath the pressure before it lurched to a halt, and the doors opened up to a room full of people who were scurrying back and forth. We got there just in time to see the thick metal guards slam closed on all of the windows in the large room and the lights slowly flicker on. There were at least fifty people scattering around in the place. It was filled with computer monitors, desks, and weapons.

The moment we stepped foot in the room, everyone around us halted and stared at us. It took me a few seconds as we walked forward to realize that they weren't staring at the guys; their eyes were locked on me.

Before I had time to ask any questions, someone from the back of the room yelled, "Brace for impact!"

I didn't need to ask any questions to know what that meant. I crouched to the floor, and everyone else did the same. I held my hands over my ears, but it still wasn't enough to cancel out the loud crash of the waves as they washed down the street. The floor rumbled and shook. I could feel the building pushing back, fighting the powerful force of nature.

The lights flickered, and the building creaked underneath the pressure. It only lasted a few seconds, but they were the longest few seconds of my life. The building finally settled into its place, and everyone raised their heads up.

A smile spread across my face. My heart was thudding, and adrenaline was racing its way through my veins. I didn't know how thrilling it was to evade death until I was thrown into the mess, but I couldn't go back to living the way I was before.

I let the excitement go to my head. I spun around and pulled the closest person to me in for a kiss—Drax. His lips pressed against mine, and I could feel the confusion on his face, but the confusion quickly melted into the kiss too. I pulled away, and the look on his face was priceless. Under normal circumstances, I didn't go around kissing people I barely knew, but it was something Scar would do. And every day that passed, every time I almost died, it was like a little piece of Scarlett died too. The old me was fading, and I didn't even know if I cared anymore. I couldn't go back to the way things were before, even if I won the trials and got to go back to my old life. The old way wasn't cutting it anymore, and I was realizing more and more that I got to choose who I could be, not anyone else.

I pulled away from Drax and left a smile plastered across his blushing face.

The man stood in front of me, stunned at what he'd just witnessed but quickly pushed it out of his mind and smiled.

"Scarlett Johnson, the National Human Rights Association would like to welcome you to its headquarters."

CHAPTER 16

The NHRA? What are they doing stationed so close to the city?

"I'm Maximus." The man held out a hand. "But my friends call me Max. You can call me Max." His mystery and whimsy had melted away, and all that was left now was his excitement to see me. It was all over his face.

I shook his hand. "It's nice to meet you?" I didn't mean for it to come out as a question, but it did anyway. I was in the vampire trials, expecting to fight for my life. The only other humans I'd expected to see were the ones that were trying to kill me. I didn't know how to process meeting ones that *didn't* want to see me dead.

"You look confused," Max's smile faded from his face. "Don't you know what's going on around the country?"

My brows pinched together, telling him everything he needed to know.

"Someone turn the broadcast on," he yelled over the commotion of everyone trying to put their desks back in place after the rumble of the water scattered papers and broke computers.

On a blank wall on the far side of the room, a projector stuttered, and a television screen appeared on the wall. A newscaster sat behind her desk in a dark purple blazer. Words in bright red letters scrolled across the news ticker at the bottom.

HISTORICALLY INHUMANE VAMPIRE TRIALS SET TO START TODAY

The woman cleared her throat.

"In somber news today, despite global push back from every major government, the historically inhumane and unethical Vampire Trials is set to commence today, a whole week before they were even scheduled to start."

The clip switched to a video of a mob protesting in Washington D.C. outside the White House. They held signs and chanted for the games to be stopped. I watched in awe; it was unlike anything I'd ever seen in my life. I'd never seen so many people pull together for something they believed in, definitely not in New York City.

The video changed to a video of me being carted out of Charlie's house in handcuffs and shoved into the back of the car. The video was shaky, and it didn't last long because an agent spotted the taper and charged after him. My heart sank just imagining whatever punishment that person must have received and what kind of fate they would suffer once they learned that they shared it with the media outside the walls.

"This year's trials has even more people in an uproar for its radical policy change, now including women in the trials, as well as the horrific slaughter that takes place afterwards known as the purge. Hundreds of protestors are marching the streets in cities across the world today, demanding an end to the barbaric practice. Our hearts and prayers go out tonight for Scarlett Johnson, the first woman to be selected."

The feed paused, and it ended with a photo of me. I stared at it blankly. It was a recent photo I had taken beside my mother after one of her treatments. I looked so different, or I felt different at least. I barely recognized the girl smiling brightly in the photo. It definitely wasn't the face of someone who just murdered another person.

The adrenaline was slowly leaving my system, and the reality of my circumstances started to settle heavy on my chest.

I killed someone. I really just killed someone.

Max seemed confused by my stunned silence, but Colt stepped forward.

"You know, she's been through a lot. Is there any way we could let her rest for a few minutes before we decide out next move?"

If I had been myself, I would have been grateful for Colt

stepping in, but I could feel myself slipping. I was spiraling, and a mental breakdown was the last thing that I needed. But it was what the trials did to you. It was a mind game meant to strip you of your humanity one phase at a time, until you started to believe that humans deserved to be purged. It made you lose faith, not only in your humanity, but everyone else's too. It was a dangerous road to go down, and once you did, there was no going back.

It threw you off your game and got you killed.

"Sure, that makes sense. Follow me."

Colt grabbed my hand and led me through the daze. We followed Max through a hallway and down a flight of stairs before he handed us each a key card. "Suites for each of you. Feel free to shower and rest. I'll send for you when we're ready to brief you."

Finn and Drax each retreated into their own room, eager to finally wash the scum of the trials off their bodies with a hot shower. Colt lead me into my room and locked the door behind us.

I turned to him, finally able to let the tears that danced in my eyes run down my cheeks. It started with a single tear before erupting into an all-out ugly cry.

"I did it. I really did what they wanted me to," I sobbed. "I killed someone in cold blood."

"Hey, hey, hey." Colt grabbed my face and held it gently between both hands. "He was trying to kill us. You did what you had to do to survive."

I sobbed so hard my body shook violently.

"This is it. I'm becoming what they wanted me to be." I could hardly see through the blur of the tears.

I thought of my father and wondered if he'd hate me for what I did. I wondered if it went against his strong moral code, if he would have disowned me for it. Then my thoughts drifted to my mother. I prayed to god that she wasn't watching the live broadcast and that their cameras hadn't caught it. Would she cry when she saw it? Would she get sick to her stomach? Either way, she'd realize that her little girl was gone, replaced by an inhumane monster. I had blood on my hands. I was as bad as the rest of them now.

My thoughts piled up and piled up until I could barely see past them anymore. I was consumed, and I couldn't find a way to dig myself out of them.

Something broke behind Colt's eyes. I knew he was reading my mind; he could feel my thoughts too. He could see I was trapped, and he didn't see a way out from underneath them either.

He pulled my face in toward his and kissed me.

The rush of his lips against mine dulled the pain and quieted my mind a little.

"Did that work?"

I looked into his eyes and saw that the pain I was feeling was destroying him too. He hated to see me like that, and I hated hurting him with my pain too.

"I don't know, do it again." I tangled my fingers in his hair and pulled him in again. I kissed him like I'd never kissed anyone before. It was full of a mix of passion and pain. The emotion danced on our tongues as they flitted together, dancing delicately in our mouths.

145

I pulled him further into the room and stumbled backwards until I could feel the bed behind my legs. I pulled him down, and he crawled between my legs before pulling away.

"How about now?"

The pain still throbbed inside of my chest. I needed more. I needed all of him to distract me, every single inch.

He nodded his head pulled his shirt from his back. I gazed up at his chiseled body, consuming every inch of his bare chest with my eyes. I devoured him in my mind, and the bulge in his pants told me he knew it. He pulled off the armor below my waist and tossed it in the corner with a *clank*. He planted a trail of kisses up my thigh before finding his way to the other thigh and working his way up to my waist. Each kiss he planted sent an electric shiver up my spine. I ached between my legs, and my body screamed for him to fill me.

"Is this working?" He looked up at me, and our eyes connected.

"It's getting there," I moaned as his tongue found its way between my legs and caressed me in all the right places. His mouth was wet and warm, and it was the best thing I'd ever felt. He flicked my clit with his tongue and a wave of pleasure flowed through my entire body. He made his way up my stomach, and I shimmied out of my chest plate.

If there was ever a time that I despised the sexy armor suit that Vinny designed for me, it was then.

Colt helped me pull it over my head, and my breasts were exposed to the brisk air. Colt pulled his pants down, and I sank my teeth into my bottom lip at the sight of him naked. I'd already devoured him with my eyes, now I was ready to devour him with my body.

Colt knelt over me, taking in every part of my body. He admired me before he leaned in and kissed me. I could taste myself on his tongue, and it drove me insane. I felt him press up against me, and he paused for a second.

"Are you sure?" He towered over me, and he clenched his jaw tightly.

"You're the mind reader, you tell me." I pulled him down into a kiss, and he pressed all of his weight against me, slipping deep inside of me. I let out of a moan as I opened up and let him into the most personal part of my body. He pumped in and out of me slowly at first, but the second I sank my nails into his back and moaned his name, he lost it. He grabbed me by the hips and fucked me as hard as he could until a wave of pleasure exploded in my mind, and we came at the same time.

He collapsed on the bed beside me, panting for air. I lay smiling in the aftermath, high off the orgasm. I watched him cool down and admired every inch of his body. I never understood the cheesy moments in the movies where the girl lay with her head on the pillow, admiring the guy, but it made more sense to me now.

"Why don't you take a picture, it'll last longer." Colt smiled and I nudged him.

"Stop," I laughed.

We cooled off for a minute before I crawled in closer to him and laid my head on his chest.

"You know he wouldn't hate you, your dad," Colt mumbled. "Your mom either. Anyone on this planet would be stupid to hate you, Scarlett Johnson."

I sighed. My mind was clear, and I knew he was right. I couldn't let the trials get to my head like that. I couldn't let them catch me at a weak moment again.

"Thanks for helping me, Colt," I smiled.

"If that's what you consider to be helping you, I'd be glad to *help* you for the rest of your life," he laughed.

I sat for a few more minutes, soaking in all the warmth that his naked body was willing to give mine. I ran my fingertips over his chest and traced the corners of his jaw.

I wanted nothing more than to stay in that moment forever, but we didn't live in a world where we could.

A vampire and a human, three vampires and a human for that matter, wasn't what the world wanted. But the more I thought about it, the more I realized it was what I wanted. I wanted all three of them, and in a world where I could defy death and change the rules of an age old game, I could get what I wanted.

CHAPTER 17

B y the time we made it out of the suite, Drax and Finn were on their way out too. They both eyed us suspiciously as I fixed my hair. I flashed an awkward smile, but I could feel my face getting hot already, so I just pushed past them both and set out on my mission to find Max. Something inside of me shifted, and the world felt a little bit hopeful. Behind me, I heard Drax, Finn, and Colt say something about finding something to eat and catching up with me later. I didn't mind exploring the headquarters alone; the architecture of the hotel was stunning. It was definitely one of the city's top hotels when it was in its prime; it was obvious. The ceilings were high and breathtaking. Renaissance paintings stretched across the hallway.

I turned a corner and felt like I could finally breathe without feeling the guys' eyes glued to me constantly. I wandered until I found myself back in the main control room. Max sat shuffling through papers at a large desk near the door. He heard my footsteps approach, and his eyes met mine. They were a pool of brown, warm and dark.

He smiled, revealing a line of straight, white teeth.

"So, you're really human," I mumbled.

"I don't know what else I'd be," he laughed. "But from what I can see, you have a tendency to gravitate toward vampires."

"I do not!" I protested. Even I was shocked at how defensive I got.

Max raised his hands. "I wasn't saying it was a bad thing. In fact, vampire and human relationships are more common than you think." He got up from his desk and motioned for me to follow him. My bruised ego told me not to, but he was handsome, and I had always been a sucker for some brown eyes.

It felt good to be around humans for once, ones that weren't trying to kill me. As much as the guys were there for me, even Finn took a bullet to keep me safe, I felt like I could breathe easier on my own here. No one here looked at me like I was fragile enough to even need someone to take a bullet for me, and I liked that.

Max looked at me like I was a Goddess, some being sent from

above to influence humanity. And the glimmer in his eye almost made me believe it.

He led me across the room to the thick metal grates that covered the windows.

"Open them up," he yelled to no one in particular. The metal plates lurched apart slowly, and I shaded my eyes from the blinding light that flooded in through them.

"Oh my god," I murmured after my eyes adjusted.

The outskirts were ravaged by the tidal wave. Most of the smaller buildings were completely lost to the water, and only the peaks of their roofs poked out. I stood in awe of the annihilation that they'd caused.

"How the hell did they do that?" I couldn't wrap my mind around how they could possibly manufacture such a destructive natural disaster.

"Witches. Elemental witches to be exact," Max said as calmly as you'd tell someone the weather.

"Witches?" I'd known they were real, but I'd never thought there were any in the city. The vampires were good at making sure they were on the top of the food chain in NYC, and witches threatened that balance. What really caught me off guard was that they thought that they needed to up their game that much and enlist in other supernatural backup just to take me out. Me, a human.

Maybe I wasn't as fragile as everyone thought. Maybe Vinny was right, and I was even kidding myself with the *just another pretty face* ruse.

"That was only phase one. We have reason to believe that they plan to use all four types of elemental witches, earth, fire, water, and air."

I didn't understand how the situation could possibly get any worse than it already was until I heard those words come out of his mouth.

"Then we have to go, now," I spun around on my heel and started off across the room to go find the guys. There wasn't any time to waste. If we were going to take this thing off the air and hijack the broadcast, we needed to do it fast. I would have rather trudged through water than push through fire, or a tornado, or whatever the hell earth witches did.

I was more ready for the trials to be over than ever before. And that wasn't even taking in to account the 6 other humans out there who wanted my head on a platter for some pathetic bribe money. I got all the way across the large room before I realized Max was trailing me close behind.

He waited until we reached the empty hallway to wrap his fingers around my wrist. "Wait." He pulled me backward. "Where are you going?"

"We have to leave now. We need to make it to the old Opera house to hijack the trials live feed. Unless, that is, you have the technology that can do that?"

"No way." Max shook his head. "They use the most outdated firmware they possibly can. Our technology isn't even compatible with theirs anymore."

I pulled my wrist from his grasp. "Like I said, we need to get out of here." I made my way back down the hall.

"What, are you in a hurry to die out there? You're not going to even ask if we have any resources for you? Are you that stubborn?"

"How do you think I stayed alive this long?" I called from down the hall.

I heard Max hesitate. I knew he was debating on whether to follow me or to let my stubborn ass figure things out on my own, an internal battle.

I knew he made a decision when I heard him do a slow jog down the hall just as I was making my way to the staircase.

He sprinted past me and positioned himself between me and the staircase. He tried to lean up against the doorway casually, but it slid open, and he almost fell backwards down the stairs. He fumbled, but he made an impressive full recovery. His cheeks turned red, but he crossed his arms and tried to look defiant.

"At least let me show you to the cafeteria. You don't want to die on an empty stomach, do you?"

My stomach growled in sync with the temptation. Max batted his big brown eyes at me, and he reminded me of a puppy begging me to play with him.

"Okay," I caved. "But then we're out."

Max looked like a kid in a candy store leading me into the cafeteria. He showed me all of the different stations it had, which was surprisingly a lot for being in the middle of an old, desolate part of the city. My stomach growled, and my mouth salivated at everything I laid eyes on. I ended up with a full tray by the time we sat down, but I didn't even care if Max saw me devour it.

I sank my teeth into a chicken leg and made eye contact at the wrong time. Max was staring at me hard core.

"I'm sorry, I just have so many questions."

I raised a brow and swallowed. "About what?"

"About life inside the walls."

It was funny because I was the one with a million questions about life *outside* of them.

"I'll make you a deal. I answer one, you answer one. Got it?"

He nodded. "Let's start with, do you have a job?"

I nodded. "My aunt is rich, and she pays me to take care of my mom. Your turn, do supernaturals and humans get along out there?"

It was my burning question, really the only question I had. I had to know if it was different somewhere out there. That there was a place in existence that humans didn't get walked on. I had to know it was possible, otherwise I didn't even know what I was fighting for.

"Totally. When the supernaturals started to rise decades ago, they integrated into society in most of the country. For some reason, New York City went bad."

Good old New York, I scoffed before digging into my food again.

"Next question, are you with that Colt guy? Or are you with Drax? Finn maybe?" Something in his eyes told me that he wasn't asking for business purposes. I doubted the information was on the *need to know* list there at headquarters. I sat quietly for a minute. Leave it to Max to ask the one question I was still asking myself.

I knew it had only been a few days since I'd met them, but I felt a deep bond to each one of the guys that I just couldn't outright explain. Maybe we were bonded by trauma; maybe we were bonded by tragedy, some might even say fate. All I knew was that I liked each of them equally, and I liked them from the start. It was a gut feeling that I had. I'd never thought I'd end up with anyone, let alone three vampire bad boys, but there I was. I wanted them all. I didn't want to choose, and there's nothing like walking the tight rope between life and your own death to make you realize that you make up the rules in your own life. My rules said that I didn't have to choose.

I felt a pull toward Max too, and I didn't know why. What I did know was that it cleared me of my fear that I was habitually attracted to supernatural, so that was a relief.

"Maybe I'm with all three," I smiled.

Max didn't flinch at the thought, and he didn't act turned off.

"Maybe one day you'll want to make it four," he smiled innocently, but it stirred something inside of me.

"I should really get going," I said, realizing I'd been auto-eating, and my tray was cleared.

The guys appeared in the doorway of the cafeteria, and I wondered if Colt had heard my thoughts and tracked me down that way.

I hoped he didn't because I was having some unholy thoughts about Max's gorgeous face.

"I'm coming with you" Max followed.

"No you're not. You're human."

"So are you. And so are the guys that are after you, so I don't see your point." Max was pretty stubborn for someone who had just accused me of being the same.

I hated it, but he had a point. If he wanted to get killed, who was I to tell him no?

"Plus I have access to a boat, which will make getting around in the 100 foot water a hell of a lot easier." He smirked.

I thought for a moment and wondered how the guys would get along. Would Finn's rough and ruggedness clash with his upbeat and excited personality? Would Colt get sick of hearing his racing thoughts all the time?

But he had a boat, and that outweighed the other concerns. My mind traveled back to my mom for some odd reason, and I wondered what she was doing. How was she holding up? Were her treatments going well?

The intrusive thoughts were welcome because they reminded me what I was fighting for. She was waiting for me to make it home, and I wasn't going to disappoint her.

"Fine." I tried to keep a straight face, but my mouth curled at the edges when I said it.

We were possibly walking straight into our deaths; what was adding one more person to the squad?

A wide smile spread across Max's face.

"I'll bring the guns."

He pushed past the guys and headed down the hall, motioning

for us to follow him excitedly.

"What, you're taking recruits for boyfriends now?" Drax joked. "I thought we were special." He feigned a sad face, and I kissed him on the cheek.

"You are, but his audition was too good to pass up," I winked, and Finn tensed up.

I had a hard time figuring out why he was upset, but I quickly dismissed it.

"Come on, guys, there's a boat with our name on it."

CHAPTER 18

I stood next to the large window on the tenth floor that they had to remove to make an exit for the building. It was just about level with the water; one more inch, and the tenth floor would have been flooded like all the floors beneath it. I was surprised when Max actually steered a small boat up to the window with a bright smile on his face. I had been having serious doubts on whether the mystery boat even existed. Members of the NHRA loaded our boat up with a few guns, some flares, and some food.

"Are you sure you don't want the whole team to come? You

have the entire NHRA at your disposal," Max said.

I shook my head. I didn't think I'd be able to handle it if any more people got hurt on my behalf. I almost lost it when Finn tried to die for me. I wouldn't have been able to forgive myself if someone with a life or a family outside of these city walls never got to go home.

We loaded into the boat and pulled out our map.

"The good news is that having a boat will cut down our travel time. The bad news is that we have no idea what is lurking in these waters. There could be downed power lines, obstacles, or god knows what kind of magical creatures the governors will pay the witches to summon. The other contenders aren't our biggest threat anymore. Now, we have to assume that the entire city is working against us." Finn laid his finger on the map. "This is the best shot we have at a quick route."

Max took the wheel of the speedboat, and it slowly lurched forward. I held my gun in my hands and sat in the back, nervously scanning every building and every window. It was safe to assume that the first phase probably took out one or two contenders; we almost didn't even make it out alive. But there were others still out there, and to them, I was just a paycheck, a payday that would set them up for life, no doubt. And in a city where you're oppressed with poverty, that was an irresistible offer. I didn't even blame them; after all, they were just trying to survive. But so was I, and every day the stakes got higher. Every day, more people were counting on me to make it out alive, and the pressure not to let them down got heavier and heavier.

"So, you really invited captain happy to come with?" Drax sat down next to me.

"He kind of invited himself, and I just went with it," I shrugged. "What? Do you have a problem with happy people?" I teased between scanning the windows, ready to squeeze the trigger if I had to.

"No, I kind of like it actually. He reminds me of me, before my life went downhill." Drax's eyes looked tired, and his face looked pale, paler than usual. He scratched at his arm, and he looked more fidgety than normal.

"Are you feeling okay?" I laid my hand on the side of his cheek. His skin was cold and clammy.

"Yeah, I'm fine. It's fine," he pulled away from my touch.

Before I could say another word, Max yelled, "Get down!" I looked up to see a small missile headed straight for the boat. Everyone flung themselves to the floor of the boat, and the missile narrowly missed the boat and crashed into the side of a random building with a loud boom. Rubble and debris flew in all directions as the building crumbled into the water beneath it. The explosion sent a surge of wild waves that shook the boat violently.

"What the hell was that?" I yelled.

I carefully pulled my head up and looked around frantically. The smoke from the explosion made it hard to tell where the missile came from in the first place. The cloud was so thick, I could barely see Max standing at the front of the small boat.

"Is everyone okay?" I yelled.

Max, Colt, and Finn all grunted their okays, but there was radio silence from Drax.

"What about Drax? Is Drax okay? I can't see him." I searched the back of the boat, and he wasn't there. My heart thudded loudly in my chest, and I started to panic. All the horrible things that could have happened while I had my back turned and was sheltering myself flashed inside my mind. For all I knew, he could have been laying at the bottom on the pit of water by now, blasted out of the boat.

"Here, here he is. I found him!" Max yelled.

Drax lay slumped over the front of the boat, just outside the small windshield. He was on his stomach and a small trickle of blood ran down his forehead. I held my breath while the guys pulled him in, still unresponsive, when a small glimmer from the window of a building across the way caught my eye.

It was so far away that I had to squint to even get a good glimpse at what it was, but when I did, my heart dropped.

"Another incoming!" I yelled just as they pulled Drax down into the boat.

I froze, and my eyes locked on the small projectile missile headed straight for us, and by the looks of this one, whoever it was launching then had been working on their aim. This time, they weren't going to miss.

A small drone emerged from behind one of the buildings, and its camera locked onto us.

My mind slowed, and it felt like time did too. Every second lasted longer than it should have, and I felt all of my emotions at once. Sadness, anger, fear, they all played well together in the playground that was my mind. I wanted to move; I needed to move, but I couldn't. All I could think about was the camera that the drone carried. I knew the trials were being live streamed, but up until then, we had done a pretty good job at evading them. Now they showed up at the exact moment of our demise, ready to stream my death to the whole world—my mother included.

I thought about the pain she would go through having to watch her daughter be blown to pieces on national television. The record of the slaughter would ring throughout history and be replayed in the trial highlights for years like all the other poor souls who lost their lives in them.

I couldn't let that happen.

Before my mind could realize what was going on, my body lunged forward and hit the gas, sending us charging straight toward the missile. The boat was fast, but the missile was faster.

I knew there was no way that we could outrun it, so our only option was to outsmart it and take out whoever it was that was launching them. The boat sped forward which sent all the guys tumbling backward, spiraling to the floor. They hung on for dear life, clinging to the seats as anchors.

My eyes caught on a large piece of debris in the water in front of us; it looked like a slab of wood or maybe even an entire section of wall from a building. All I knew was that it was at the perfect angle to use as a jump. To be completely honest, I didn't even know if it was possible to jump a speedboat, but we were about to find out. It was better than just laying down and dying. If I was going to die on national television, I was going to do it in a blaze of fury, fighting until the very end. I was going to show my mother that she raised a fighter, just like her.

I smiled at the thought.

And if I was wrong, I was going to see my dad again, and at that point, either one was fine with me.

"Brace yourselves," I screamed.

Colt wrapped his arm around Drax and anchored himself to him. The boat jerked violently as it crashed into the debris. The missile was so close now that I swore I could hear it gliding through the air. I could almost feel the heat radiating off of its blast. The boat soared into the air. I held my breath as we climbed higher and higher, just high enough to jump over the missile just as it lowered into the water where the boat once was. There was a huge splash that sent water projectile firing in all directions. There was a huge explosion behind us, but I didn't even care anymore. I pulled my gun, and we sped straight in the direction that the missile came from. There was another glint up ahead. I could finally see where it was coming from: one of the top floor windows of an old executive building.

"There you are, you bastard," I mumbled before letting go of the gas and pulling the scope up to my eye. I saw the man frantically trying to reload a missile into his launcher. I took a deep breath and tried to slow the jitters I had in my hands from the adrenaline. I remembered what my father had taught me when he was teaching me how to shoot; always line it up and breathe first. If you hold your breath, you get sloppy.

I closed the trigger, and the bullet struck him. He must have accidentally launched the missile because there was a huge explosion in the building that busted out most of the windows.

The drone above us lowered itself, and its camera gleamed.

"Suck on that Governor." I flipped it off before I raised my gun and shot the drone too. I got a sick sense of satisfaction just knowing how much that would get under the governor's skin. I hoped that the entire city had seen it; the entire world would have been even better. I wanted every person who supported the games to hear loud and clear that I was there to take them down, and I wasn't going to let anything stop me.

"Scar, we have a problem," Colt said. He stared at the map.

I looked at him and tilted my head.

"We're here".

"What do you mean we're here?"

"That was the opera building." He pointed toward the crumbling executive building. Most of it was under water and what wasn't under water was up in flames."

Fuck.

"Okay. Okay, Okay, Okay," I thought out loud. "Drax is out cold, and he's really the only one with random knowledge about the outskirts and its abandoned buildings. So, what would he do?"

I grabbed the map and searched it frantically. "Here," I pointed to a point on the map that showed higher ground, a prison. It sat on a large hill just outside of the outskirts. The water probably wasn't high enough to reach it, and it was a good place to regroup and figure out how the hell we were going to hijack a television signal with absolutely no equipment. Plus, Drax wasn't looking too good. We needed to get him to some place safe to recover; being out on the water like sitting ducks was just going to get us killed. With an explosion that loud, every contender was going to gravitate to the area. We had to get out of there, and we had to do it fast.

"Hold on everyone." I reached for the steering wheel, but I felt Max's hand rest gently on my shoulder.

"Actually, do you mind if I drive?" He smiled awkwardly. "I kind of want us to make it there alive, you know?"

My mouth hung open, and Max laughed.

"The nice guy's got jokes," Finn laughed in the background.

I crossed my arms, nursing my bruised ego.

"Can we just go?" I moaned, but deep down I liked that Max was getting more comfortable; maybe he could turn out to be one of the guys after all.

CHAPTER 19

I t didn't take us long to make it to the prison that was just outside of town. The water was as high there as it was everywhere else, but luckily, the prison sat on top a large hill, too high for the water to reach. We anchored the boat at the bottom of the hill and climbed out onto a dirt road that wove up the hill and to the prison. Max and Finn helped cart a still unconscious Drax out of the boat and each helped carry him up the hill with his arms slung around their shoulders.

Colt and I carried the supplies. The hill was a lot steeper than I anticipated, and I wondered how any cars ever even made it up the old road.

"Are you sure we can trust this guy?" Colt asked. The question made me uneasy; it wasn't like Colt not to trust someone, or at least try to see the good in them.

"You're the one that can read minds, you tell me," I whispered back.

The last thing I wanted to do was put anyone else in any more danger than I already had. I didn't want any re-runs of the Bobby situation, but I also didn't want to shut anyone out. It was a constant war that raged on inside of me.

Colt was about to say something when there was a loud rushing sound, like when the tidal wave came through.

"Oh no." I froze. I expected to see another huge wave coming straight for us, but instead, all of the water was receding. It was flowing back to wherever it came from in huge waves. Our boat now sat in the middle of the surprisingly dry, gravel road.

I looked at Colt with a smile on my face. "That's good right?"

A wave of hope finally started to flow through me. Maybe we would make it out of there after all.

Colt shook his head. "That just means we survived phase one. There are three more to go."

There was a light buzzing overhead. I squinted to try to see it on the horizon. The most annoying thing about the trials was all the stupid drones, always trying to catch video of us. Like the people of New York City didn't have anything better to do than watch us kill each other and eventually ourselves.

I finally spotted the drone, and my heart stopped. It wasn't a normal camera drone; this one had ammo blasters strapped to it.

"Go, go, go, go, go!" I yelled.

Up ahead, Max and Finn didn't even ask why; they just broke out into a full sprint. A spray of automatic bullets showered down behind us. I whispered a silent thank you to the universe for technology lag and ran as fast as I could. Up ahead, the prison came into view. I couldn't grab my weapon because it was tangled up in all the other supplies that I held unsteadily in my hands.

We finally made our way to the gates and pushed through them. The drone let out another spray of bullets, and a red hot pain sliced through my arm. I didn't think. I just reacted, dropping all of the supplies on the ground. I stopped to grab them, but Colt grabbed me by the arm, pulling me out of reach of another spray of bullets just in time. Up ahead, the guys had already made it inside the cement building and were standing in the doorway motioning for us to come inside. We ran as fast as we could and sprinted through the doorway. Max shoved the thick steel door tightly closed. We could hear the spray of bullets slamming against the door, but it was secure enough to keep them out.

"Are you okay?" Max grabbed my arm.

"Yeah, it's just a surface wound. We need to focus on Drax." I made my way to his body slumped in the corner and shook him, but I didn't get a response.

"This is a prison. Prisons have infirmaries, right? We need to wake him up."

"She's right." Finn backed me up. "Phase one is over, which means phase two is on its way. And the drone knows where we are, which means soon, every contender that's left in the trials will too. If we're not ready, we're toast."

I was a little surprised that Finn jumped at the chance to have my back, but my worry for Drax trumped everything else at that moment. I carried what was left of the supplies so Colt could help carry Drax. We made our way out of the dust-covered waiting area and managed to pry the door open that lead back into the holding cell and inmate areas. Just like the hotel, everything was covered in a thick layer of dust that made my lungs scratchy with every breath I took. We finally found the infirmary, which was really just a glorified closet that had a cot and a few straggling bits of medical supplies left. They flopped Drax's body down on the cot, and Colt rummaged through the medical supplies.

"Smelling salts." He pulled out a tiny white stick and broke it in two before waiving it underneath Drax's nose. After a few seconds, his eyes popped open, and he sat straight up.

"Where the hell am I?" His eyes were wide. It took him a second of looking around the room frantically before his memory started to slowly seep back in.

"I'm not dead?" he smiled.

"No, just having withdrawals." Max said matter-of-factly. "What was it, ice? Or something stronger?"

"Max." I scolded, but Drax held up a hand stopping me.

"Ice," he said quietly.

It made sense now, the shivers and cold sweats, clammy skin. The guy practically jumped at every noise over the last few days. I should have made the connection. It was no secret that Drax liked to party, and I was positive he was an alcoholic, but the thought of him doing ice never occurred to me. That was a grade A, hardcore, magical drug.

A small piece of me felt sad at the defeat in his voice, especially now that I had gotten to know him more. His story was tragic; it was no wonder he turned to drugs and drinking.

"How about let's give him some air?" I asked. "We can go raid the building for weapons and make sure that it's locked down. The others are on their way; there's no doubt about it. The question is whether or not we'll be ready for it."

The guys nodded and started to file out one by one.

"Wait, Scar, will you stay?" Drax called out from the cot. I turned to look at him, and his big eyes melted my heart. Who would have known that triad three's prince of mischief could ace the puppy dog eyes perfectly?

"Yeah," I said and closed the door.

I rummaged through the cupboards and found some medical wipes and sat down next to him. "No offense, but you're looking rough," I joked.

"None taken. I feel rough." He winced at the antiseptic wipe's sting against the small cut on his forehead. "You must think I'm some hardcore drug bum."

"Hardcore drug bum," I snorted. "That's the first time I've ever heard that one before. I must be really behind on the vampire terms.

Drax cracked a smile and some of the weight in my chest lifted. It hurt to see him hurt. I didn't necessarily understand how or why I'd bonded so quickly to the guys, but I did. And seeing any one of them hurt, no matter how big and bad they thought they were, didn't sit right with me.

I dabbed a cut on the side of his temple, and my eyes gravitated toward his. They were like two deep pools of sadness. I wondered what it was that was torturing him, but Drax was the type of person that hated to feel dependent on someone else. He hated talking about his emotions, so he bottled them all up and trapped them inside. Maybe the only way he could let some of the pressure out was drinking. Maybe drugs were the only thing that made him feel alive. I wanted to know. I had to know. But there was only one way that I knew I would get a truthful answer.

I leaned in close and kissed him softly. Our lips brushed against one another's so lightly that it was like they were taking part in a delicate dance. But it was just enough contact for his power to kick in. Images flooded my mind of Drax. He stood in a party, surrounded by people that partied and smiled, but he looked so alone. I was drenched in a wave of loneliness that crept into every crevice of my soul. His emotions became mine, and I felt like I was drowning in a sea that I could never swim my way out of. I watched him down drinks, and with each one he swallowed, I felt a little more numb. I watched him do every kind of drug known to man, and by the time he was done, I felt nothing, which was a step up from the pit of despair that I felt before. Then an image of him now popped into my head. Him with his lips pressed against mine, and I felt something different. Something warm and something fuzzy. The complete opposite of the cold and desolate loneliness of before.

I pulled away and looked him in the eyes. "Is that how I make you feel?"

He nodded.

"Then let's do it again." I smiled and pulled his face into mine. My lips devoured his. It was like he was air, and I just came up from near suffocation. I couldn't get enough. My hands roamed his body, feeling every single inch of it, and I smirked at the gasps he let out. Images flooded my mind every time I touched a part of his body. Pieces of his past, things from his present. I was learning more about him in those moments than I had over the last few days, and I wanted more. I needed to know more of his body, and I needed to know more of his past.

He sank a fang into my bottom lip, and a small drop of blood beaded from it. He licked it off, and it drove me crazy. My clit screamed for attention between my legs, to which he happily obliged. I couldn't tell if the fireworks in my head were his or mine, but I didn't care anymore. I pulled him in close, and he pulled himself between my legs. Sometime during the process, my armor had come off, and I lay exposed on the prison cot. His mouth found its way to my nipple, and he nibbled on it gently.

"God, I want you inside me," I moaned.

172

"Your wish is my command." He looked down at me with a mischievous grin.

He pumped in and out of me, taking me to new heights of pleasure. I was ravenous for his dick, and he was just as ravenous for me.

"I'm almost there; I'm almost there," I moaned, sinking my fingernails into his back before I reached the peak of my ecstasy.

He collapsed beside me, and I stared at the ceiling with my signature sex smile plastered across my face.

I looked at him and sighed.

This could work, I thought. *Maybe I can be his new drug.*

I laid my head on his bare chest, and his power transferred what he was feeling to me—love.

CHAPTER 20

I had just slipped back into my armor by the time that Max burst through the door with some weapons and supplies. He eyed Drax and I suspiciously, but I just smirked.

"We should be safe here for a while. With all the water gone, it's going to take the others a lot longer to reach us on foot," Max said.

His words were a relief. I was so sick of running and so tired of looking over my shoulder. I didn't want to have to kill anymore, not unless I absolutely had to. The first time was rough. It was hard, and it almost broke me. The second time was a lot easier, and instead of making me feel better, that made me feel worse. I didn't want to know what the third time would feel like or the fourth. Eventually, would it stop feeling bad all together?

Was that how the governors conditioned the vampires of the city? If you legalize killing and normalize it enough, it stops feeling like a crime and starts to feel more and more like a right.

And it was a right that I didn't want to exercise anymore.

"Did you find anything useful?" I raised a brow.

"Maybe," Max motioned for us to follow him.

We made our way out into the hallway, and the electricity slowly flickered on.

"Good, Colt got the generator working. I didn't know if the engines would still fire because it was so old," Max said.

He sounded like he knew what he was talking about. He actually seemed super comfortable in the chaos that surrounded us. It was hard not to be suspicious. A human that wasn't from New York and hadn't been conditioned to the trauma that we had in the city would have been freaking out, whether they were part of the Human Rights Association or not, nothing would prepare them for this. I couldn't help but wonder, who was Maximus really. And why did he show up just when we needed him most?

I hated that the trials made me question things like that, but I didn't know what his motives were and that was what scared me the most. I didn't know who he was, or where he came from, but I wasn't going to put another person in jeopardy until I found out.

"Hey Drax, do you think you could go find Colt and let him

know that we have some spare weapons in the infirmary?"

We stopped walking for a minute, and Drax looked at me, confused. I wanted to tell him that I needed to be alone with Max to dig up dirt, but that was the sort of thing you tried not to say while he was right behind you.

I pulled Drax in for a kiss. Our lips touched, and I knew my thoughts transferred to him. Something behind his eyes clicked, and when I pulled away, he smiled.

"Yeah, I can track him down. You guys be careful." He didn't take his eyes off of mine. He said it, and I knew he meant it.

Drax was a bad boy. He like to party and drink and enjoy the moment, but he was fragile too, and he knew it. Something told me that he didn't let people in very often, and he wouldn't know what to do if something happened to the one person he finally decided to show the real him to.

I nodded and watched as Drax walked away, disappearing around a corner. I nodded to Max, and he kept leading me through the halls.

The old cement walls were cracked, but they still stood sturdily. With just Max and I, I realized how eerie the building really was. It gave off some majorly haunted vibes, but ghosts were the last thing on my mind. Uncovering Max's ghosts was on the top of my list. What kind of skeletons did he have in his closet?

We passed a row of empty cells, and a shiver ran down my spine at the site.

"I wonder who they kept here. What kind of criminals were

they?" I thought out loud. Questions like that crossed my mind often.

"There weren't any criminals here. Only supernaturals," Max answered. "A long time ago, at the beginning of the takeover when the supernatural creatures had enough of hiding in the dark shadow that humanity cast, they came out of the dark, and humans, in natural human fashion, condemned them to places like this. Concentration camps for creatures of the night, essentially. There are even small cells across the building for the children that they deemed too dangerous to be walking the streets. Vampires, werewolves, witches, none were spared."

What? My stomach churned at the thought. "Why didn't I know that?" I muttered.

"Because it's not something that humanity is proud to share. You'll find a lot of those things scattered throughout history."

He had a point, and I was the first person to admit humanity's faults, but he said the words like he wasn't part of the humanity that was the problem.

I searched my mind for more questions that would help reveal more of who he was. I didn't dare call him out until I had enough suspicion. Maybe I was just broken, scarred from Bobby's betrayal.

We turned a dusty corner and walked into an old surveillance room. Old computer screens were in the process of rebooting from the recent surge of power.

"Good, they're starting up," Max sighed. "I think this is our best bet at hijacking their broadcast. It uses the same type of technology that they do to broadcast the trials. Since the opera house is out of commission, we need to work with what we've got."

For a minute, interrogating Max flew out the window, and I remembered what kind of deep shit we were really into. My stomach twisted at the thought of having to go on air in front of millions of people. What would I even say? What words could come out of my mouth that would possibly be strong enough to influence an entire nation? What could I say that would possibly convince all of the oppressed people of New York to rise up and fight back?

A wave of anxiety swept through me and settled into my bones.

"Hey," Max noticed me spiraling and took a step closer. With him that close, I noticed the small specks of gold that were imbedded in his deep brown eyes. It reminded me of chocolate melting in the warm rays of the sun. A liquid pool that I'd love to dive deep into. "Take a deep breath."

"I'm not nervous," I protested.

"You're definitely nervous. But you have no need to be." He smiled softly and took another step closer. His body was so close that I could feel his warmth radiating from it. There was something about him that was electric. Like a static that clung to his own personal atmosphere. He had an aura than oozed mystery and intrigue, and I didn't know how much I liked a little a mystery until one stood in front of me in the form of a man.

"Well, that's nice of you to say," my voice went soft. "But I don't know how true it is." My voice grew to only a whisper as he slowly leaned in. Our lips were only inches apart, and I could feel wisps of his warm breath brush against my lips.

I felt the electricity sparking between both of us, and I was having a hard time telling if it was just metaphorical or not anymore. Something about Maximus drew me in like a magnet. Something about him kept me coming back. It was like our auras fed off of each other's, and I wanted to know more. I needed to know more, even if it killed me.

"Who are you?" I asked straight out. Dancing around the subject was getting me nowhere.

"I'm Maximus," he smiled.

The door next to us burst open, and the three guys stumbled into the room awkwardly.

"We were definitely not listening at the door," Drax chuckled and rubbed at the back of his neck.

I didn't realize that Max's body was pressed completely against mine until he quickly moved away.

"Do you think this will be enough to hijack their signal?" Max asked Drax.

He examined the equipment closely to make sure everything still ran.

"It could work," he mumbled. "I saw a room set up down the hall that they must have used to let prisoners video chat. We could use that as a carrier for the signal. But we need to do it fast. We don't know when the second phase is going to start, and we need to get this message sent out fast. I'm less concerned about the rest of the country, but we need to make sure that the people of New York are able to see it."

I nodded and followed Drax down the hall. He led me into a small cement room that held a single metal table and a sturdy chair. And old video camera sat strapped to a tripod.

I sat in the chair awkwardly and watched him work. He went to work on the camera, pressing buttons and plugging in chords.

"It's a surprise that any of this stuff even works anymore, it's been so long," I mumbled.

"Ten years isn't that long," Drax mumbled.

"Ten years?" I swallowed. "That can't be right, can it? In school, they always told us that the outskirts had been abandoned a long time ago, before the wall was built."

"If it was abandoned, why would they feel the need to build a wall to separate it from the rest of the city?" Drax looked up from his work and saw the confusion on my face. "I'm sorry, I thought that it was just something everyone knew. It makes sense that they told you that though. The outskirts were the only part of the city where supernaturals and humans vowed to live in harmony. It was a threat to their way of life, so the governors," he paused. "...Our fathers fucked it up, like they do with everything they touch." There was a sour note buried deep within his voice.

Before I could say another word, he walked out of the room to connect the signal to the towers outside of the prison, or something super smart like that. It never ceased to amaze me what wonders went on inside his head below the shallow surface of drugs and partying. It made me wonder where he would have ended up if none of this had ever happened. If the governors weren't pure evil piles of shit, and he had grown up in a loving home, he probably would have worked in IT. Maybe he would have created an app or started a company. With that brain of his, anything was possible; it was just hard for him to navigate his trauma to see it.

I heard him, Colt, and Finn outside the door talking about wire connections or something when Max found a way to sneak in. He leaned up against the table and smiled.

"You can do this, okay? The people in this country have been looking for a savior. A silver lining. Something good to come from the horrible things that have happened in New York for decades; that can be you. In today's political climate, they're looking for someone who can unite both sides of the spectrum- supernaturals and humans. Even in the rest of the country, it's been like you have to choose a side; you can never just choose both. We haven't had a human member of the presidential cabinet since the takeover, and the scales are all wrong. They're either tipped one way, or they're tipped the other. It's time that we had someone even them out."

Once again, Max opened his mouth, and I couldn't get a good read on him. Sometimes, he gave off the vibe that he wasn't being totally honest, which set off my inner truth meter, and other times, he was being so authentic that I didn't know how to handle it.

"Are you ready?" Drax popped his head into the room. "Their firewall was sloppy at best. You can tell they didn't think anyone was smart enough to do this, so they got lazy."

My chest tightened, and my breathing got quicker. It was like all my anxiety had found a way to slither up my body and wrap around my heart. All I felt was squeezing.

Max laid his hand on mine. "All they have to do is see you. So far, all the exposure that they've gotten of you came from tabloids and news articles. You have a good two minutes before the governors' team takes us off air. You don't have to be perfect, and you don't have to be fearless, you just have to be real."

I nodded and moved a strand of hair from my face. Max closed the door and gave me a thumbs up through the dingy window. I took a deep breath, and the small red light above the lens blinked on. We were live streaming.

I thought of my mother, and my father, and Charlie, and every single person who had lost their lives over the years. This wasn't my chance to say what I wanted to say; this was a chance to say what they couldn't.

"Hey world. My name's Scarlett, and I'm from triad three."

CHAPTER 21

It was weird talking to a camera. It felt stale and awkward, but what Drax and Max had said was enough to light a fire of passion inside of me that I didn't even care anymore.

"I'm sure by now that everyone knows I was the first woman selected to be a contender in the vampire trials, and it's caused a chain reaction that rippled through the country. To that I say, it's about damn time. How long did it take for the rest of the country to wake up? Where were you when innocent men were being slaughtered? What makes it so atrocious now that someone with a vagina is going to be killed?" I nearly shocked myself with the word, but at that point, the words were just flowing, there wasn't anything I could do to stop them anymore. Years of being walked on and treated like we were nothing but a food source was spilling over now, and the words were running out of my mouth like they were water. "To everyone out there who's cheering me on and showing their support for my survival, I thank you, but it is not enough. There is power in numbers, and the more of you who oppose the game publicly, the more power there is. And to the people in New York, don't fall for the mind games. They divided us into triads to do just that, make us feel divided. To make us forget that there are more of us in the city than there are of them. They knew that if we banded together, they wouldn't have a chance to keep us in bondage. Which is why I don't just vow to win this sadistic ritual, I vow to end it. Humans and supernaturals will live in harmony, or none of us will live at all."

The red light on the camera shut off, and I sighed.

Max slowly clapped as he entered the room, and I was just coming down from the high of adrenaline that still raced through my veins.

"Do you think it'll work? Are my words really enough to start a citywide riot and topple a supernatural regime?"

"Well, we're just going to have to find out." Max was only inches from my body, and every inch of me tingled again. I couldn't tell if it was from him or the shock of what I'd just done, but I liked it. And I liked that I liked him. I was starting to feel like a hypocrite—a walking contradiction for falling for so many vampires, the very creatures that I swore that I hated.

Emotions were running high, and I didn't know if I was going to live to see another day, so I pulled him in for a kiss. He looked surprised and scared all wrapped up into one. I was too fast for him to pull away, but when our lips connected, there was a woosh of cool air that ran through my body and sucked the air from my lungs. My eyes widened, and I pulled away. "What the hell was that?" I brought my fingers to my lips.

Suddenly, the room started to shake so violently that I could feel it through the floor. Beneath us, something rumbled, and far off, a siren sounded.

It was time for phase two.

We sprinted through the halls, dodging falling chunks of cement and falling debris until we found the others.

"We need to get out of here. Fast! This thing is like a death trap waiting to collapse on us," I yelled over the rumbles. Suddenly, the mystery that was Maximus was the farthest thing from my mind.

A huge chunk of the ceiling crashed to the floor and created a solid wall of rubble between them and us. I choked and gagged on the cloud of dust that engulfed us. It tasted like a mixture of stale dirt and mold.

"Oh my god, are you guys okay?" I coughed.

"Yeah, we're okay. We just need to find a way out of here, fast." Colt's voice was faint. "We'll meet you outside."

Max grabbed me by the hand, interlocking his fingers with mine before pulling me away from the destruction. "This way," he coughed.

He dragged me along the hallways as the shaking started to settle.

"What the hell was that?" I said between gasps for fresh air.

We stumbled through an open doorway, and he had to kick in the front door in order for it to open past the large pile of debris that fell in front of it.

"That was an earth witch." Max bent over to catch his breath. "A super powerful one by the feel of it."

Just as the guys looped around to find us from the back exit, an arrow soared through the air and sliced right into Max's neck. His eyes opened wide, and he froze.

I didn't even realize that a blood curdling scream escaped my lips nearly shattering my own ear drums. Max's body lay on the ground and he choked and writhed.

Tears streamed down my face, and I saw red. I'd never in my life felt as angry as I did in that very moment as I charged forward, gun first. I shot anything and everything that moved in a fit of blind rage. I didn't know why I was so upset, but I was. I hadn't felt a hurt like that in a long time. A drone flew above me, but I didn't care. I wanted them to get it on camera. I wanted them to see what I was capable of. But most of all, I wanted them to pay for taking my mystery away from me.

The man with the bow threw it to the ground and pulled out a gun. He was quick, but I was quicker. I didn't know how, but I was able to squeeze my trigger before he could and struck him down quickly.

I turned to the drone that hovered closely and screamed, "I'm coming for you next!" I screamed at the machine before aiming directly at the camera and blowing it to pieces.

Drax, Colt, and Finn all rushed to my side, but I pushed them away.

"He's gone," Colt said as I stumbled to Max's side.

He lay there, cold and blue.

"We can't just leave him here to be eaten by animals." I snapped. They looked at each other, but no one had the heart to argue with me. The other contenders would be closing in soon. We didn't have time for arguments. So Colt and Finn picked him up and carried him with us.

"Where the hell do we go now? What do we do? We know this is retaliation because of the broadcast. I'd be surprised if they didn't just nuke the whole city and call it a night," I rambled to Drax who did his best to keep me on track.

"Well, it would help if we knew what was coming next. Phase one was water, phase two was earth, all that are left are fire and air. But those are two completely different things. It's hard to shelter if we don't know which one it is that we're sheltering from."

A light when off in my head.

"The subway system. What about that? The city is dry now so we don't have to worry about flooding, any air attack like a tornado can't get us if we're underground, and what's going to start on fire in an old subway?"

Drax looked at me out of the corner of his eye. "You'd be surprised some of the things that I've seen start on fire that weren't supposed to be flammable in the first place. It all depends on how good the party is."

I smiled through my tears. I could totally imagine Drax with a glass of bourbon in one hand and a lighter in the other, dancing until the sun came up.

"She's got a point," Colt grunted, but I was sure he was just agreeing with me so we could stop for rest, and they could finally put down Max's dead weight—no pun intended.

Drax pulled the map from his pocket and spun it around a few times searching for the prison and the nearest subway entrance.

"There," he pointed at the map. "It's just around the corner."

Drax led us down the tall hill and into the main part of the city. The day was slowly fading into afternoon, and it seemed like the sun hung lower and lower in the sky with every step I took.

Just as we reached the intersection across from the subway entrance, there was a loud noise down the street. It sounded like heavy machinery and not for construction. Drax pulled us into a nearby alley, and Colt and Finn set Max's body down propped against the wall to catch their breath. The sound was so loud, it was almost deafening.

What is that? I peeked around the corner just slightly enough to see a huge military tank barreling down the street.

"Go, go, go!" I pushed the guys back into the alleyway. I could tell by the sound that it was on its way toward us and fast. If the driver spotted us, it was over. We were finished, and the trials lived to see another day.

"Here, this way." I ripped open the alleyway door just in time to for us all to slip inside as the tank turned down out street.

I breathed a sigh of relief in the dimly lit building. I looked around; it was a small, old timey barber shop. It even had the blue and red spinner out front. There was only one room in the entire building, and it was the main one. Barber chairs lined either side of the mirrored walls, and I tried my hardest not to look at my reflection. I didn't know how fragile of a state I was in; the last thing I wanted was to see my reflection and start balling.

Colt and Finn laid Max gently on the ground.

"So, what, are they scrambling the military on us now too?" I groaned, trying to keep my eyes from landing on Max's body. "Why? What do they get from that? They already have us killing each other off one by one; what else could they possibly want?"

"More power," Max groaned, sitting up.

I screamed and jumped backward, noticing the wound on his neck was completely healed. "What the hell!"

The guys looked uneasy too as they each took a step back. Internally, I fought hard between being happy that Max was even breathing and wanting to shoot him in the head for still being alive.

I pulled my gun from my holster and aimed it at his gorgeous face.

"You didn't answer me before, but you will now. Who the fuck are you?" I glared down the barrel of the gun at him.

CHAPTER 22

M ax erupted in a fit of coughing and rubbed at the smooth skin of his throat. There wasn't a bruise, cut, or scar in sight.

"Man, that always stings like a bitch." He coughed again before he shot both hands in the sky, finally recognizing the rage in my eyes.

Lied to again by someone I decided to trust, even though no other sane person would. The joke was on me, and I didn't think that it was an ounce funny. Not even a little.

I raised a brow at his silence. I was no longer accepting silence as an answer.

"I knew something was up when I couldn't read his mind," Colt said quietly. "And I couldn't put my finger on it, but his face looked so familiar."

I turned quickly to Colt.

"Sorry I didn't have much time to mention it while we were busy running for our lives," he said, answering my question before it could even come out of my mouth.

Fair enough. But I'm still pissed.

"Please don't say it," Max pleaded. "Once the words come out of your mouth, everything changes. I want to be a nobody, just let me."

"You better not. Tell me, Colt. Now." I stared at him with fire in my eyes. "All I know is someone better start talking, and they better start now," I yelled.

"What do you want to know?" Max sighed.

"Let's start with your name and end with everything else. Including whatever supernatural creature you are," I demanded.

"My name really is Maximus. Maximus Finch. I swear, the only thing I lied about was being human. Nothing else was a lie."

His words were empty and meaningless. My trust for him was slipping further and further away with every second that passed, and if he lied, he better have a damn good reason. I prayed that he chose his next words closely because in that moment, I realized that something inside of me was broken. The games cracked my moral compass, and I couldn't be sure that I trusted myself not to pull the trigger. I was in survival mode, and all it took was one more lie to shatter me completely. There was something deep inside me that the trials had surfaced, something that I didn't want to believe was a part of me. It was like a shadow. A dark and seductive side that I didn't even know that I had, but now that I did? There was no going back. The old Scarlett was dead, and there wasn't a spell in the world that could resurrect her.

"Tell her the whole story of who you are," Colt said protectively. I had to pretend like his overprotective nature didn't send shivers between my legs. There were more pressing matters at hand.

Max sighed, and his face contorted like it was actually painful for the next words to come out of his mouth. "My name is Maximus Finch, and my father is Lincoln Finch. He's a witch and," he paused. "The President of the United States." The words caught me off guard. They shocked me like a slap in the face. I stood speechless for a second as the words sunk in. "So you're like, the Frist Son, or something?"

Max held in a laugh, and I couldn't tell if that made things better or worse. "No one actually calls me that, like, ever. But if that's what you want to call it." He shrugged his shoulders.

"But why? Why lie?" I was confused at what he gained from keeping his identity a secret. What did he get out of any of this? "Do you even work for the NHRA, or was that a lie too?" I snapped.

"Of course I do, I wouldn't lie about something like that. I'm not a monster."

"Just a witch."

Max shrugged his shoulders at the statement, but I could tell by the look on his face that the way I said it stung.

I slowly lowered by weapon and groaned.

"Would you have accepted my help right away if you knew who

I was? That my father was a witch, one with the most political power in the country at that?"

I rolled my eyes, but the truth was I didn't know the answer to that. I didn't know what I would have done, or if I would have trusted him. I barely trusted myself anymore; the trials were fucking with my head in the worst ways. "Scarlett, I didn't mean any harm, okay? My father didn't know where I was, and it wasn't something I wanted televised. Not until the right time." "Well look at where that got you. Killed on National Television."

Max smirked. "Exactly."

"Wait what?" I looked at him out of the corner of my eye.

"You smart bastard!" Finn almost screamed.

"Oh my god, you're bloody brilliant." Colt made the connection too.

Drax and I stared blankly at one another. We clearly weren't getting whatever the other two were.

"I knew you wouldn't know who I was. We know that television and internet access is extremely restricted by the governors in New York. They like to pretend they're the only ones with power in the entire world, so I hoped that you'd let me come with you. Traveling with you, it was only a matter of time before I'd get killed." "Oh great, use my trauma to make yourself a target. But how did you come back?"

"Cursed as a baby to live an eternity of misery," he said casually. "It's a long story. But I hoped that when it happened, the drone would be there and capture it. No one else knows about the curse but my mother and I, rest her soul. Can you imagine the outrage that the magical citizens of America must be feeling right now? I'm America's sweetheart." He flashed a goofy smile. "And I just died at the hands of a human in the Vampire Trials. It's basically as bad as dying at the hands of one of the governors themselves."

"Oh my god, that is genius." I could help it, the praise just fell out of my mouth before my brain could process a single word. I didn't know if I was pissed at him or not anymore, but I wasn't going to off him like an animal. I slid my gun back into my holster. "The entire country is probably on fire right now, huh?" "That and the White House." Max got to his feet and brushed a layer of dust from his coat.

The storm inside me settled, and the anger came to a still. I had bigger fish to fry at the moment. I could give Max hell once we both made it out alive.

There was another loud rumbling outside of the barber shop, and I quietly moved to the window. "Another tank? What the hell is going on? I'd never heard of the governors scrambling military forces during the trials before."

"Those don't belong to the Governors," Max said quietly. "There's a United States Magical Military base nearby. They're coming to enter the city, not out of it."

"Wait? Does that mean it worked?" I cranked my head to see it head further down the street toward the wall that separated the city from the outskirts.

"They're here to rip the walls down, and hopefully rip the governors apart," Max said it with a sick satisfaction before flinching at the statement, realizing that he was talking about the guys' dads. "Sorry," he mumbled.

The guys just shrugged, but I knew somewhere deep down, they had to be having some sort of emotions about everything going on. No matter how toxic a parent is, you have to have some sort of attachment. Even if it was a dysfunctional one. I made a mental note to check in with them later when this was all over. But we had to figure out our next move, and we had to do it fast. Everything was exploding right in front of me, and all I knew was that I had to survive long enough to get my mom and get out of the city. I didn't care where we went, or if we ever found our way back to New York. I wanted to see the city, and the trials, in my rear view mirror, and I wasn't looking back.

"So what do we do now?" Drax asked.

"It's simple. We get to the governors before anyone else does. I want them to look me in the face as they realize their system is broken. I want them to see the face that changed their world. I don't care what happens after." The fire inside me was blazing once again.

"Are we sure that's a good idea?" Drax's eyes filled with fear. Some people would consider Drax a monster. A big scary vampire with a drug problem. But what do you call the monster that the monster is afraid of?

"It's the best I've got. But how do we make it happen?"

"The subway systems," Drax mumbled, almost like he was fighting himself to get the words out, unsure if he even wanted to say them or not. "They connect the two cities together. There's no telling what's down there, but it's our fastest way in. Especially with the military knocking on their doors. If we do it right, they'll never see us coming."

I nodded. The plan sounded easy, almost too easy. But if I'd learned anything from the trials, it was that nothing that seemed easy ever was. The nearest subway entrance was just around the corner, but we had to figure out how to get through without being seen.

A sudden wave of fatigue swept over me, and I realized that I didn't remember the last time I'd rested. My body betrayed me by letting out a yawn, and the sun outside began to set.

"Why don't we rest for a bit? There's no way we're toppling an empire running on E." Colt read my mind, yet again. "I noticed a small door that leads to the upstairs apartment above this place." He gestured toward the corner where a small door sat.

I didn't want to rest. I wanted to fight and scream and resist injustice all at the same time. But I knew he was right. There was no way we were getting anywhere while I was tired and drained.

I nodded reluctantly. There was another rumble headed our way, so we quickly made our way up the small staircase. It was just narrow enough for one of us to fit at a time, and every step we took sent a cloud of dust into the air. At the top of the steps, we found an old two bedroom apartment. I was surprised that an apartment that big could fit above such a small barber shop. I wondered how they'd found the space to fit a living room, kitchen, and two bedrooms above it, but I wasn't about to complain.

We rounded up all the blankets and strung them up over the windows to keep anyone from seeing through the windows. When we were done, I felt like I could finally breathe again. Like maybe we'd finally found a bit of a safe haven, even if it was only for an hour or two. I breathed a sigh of relief at the king sized bed in one of the rooms. It called my name like a siren leading a sailor to his death. I didn't care how old or dusty it was; it looked like a slice of heaven served up on a silver platter for me to devour. I unloaded the few supplies we were able to bring with us, which included an old stale can of baked beans. I didn't care though; they tasted like a five course meal.

"Get some rest." Colt said as he passed by the room in the hallway. "We'll keep guard."

He didn't have to tell me twice. My world faded to black the second my head hit the pillow.

CHAPTER 23

I don't know how long I was asleep for, just that I woke up in a panic. One of those panics you have on a Saturday morning where you wake up in a pure sweat, afraid you'd missed the bus for school until you remember that you're twenty and haven't been to school in years. My heart raced, but my mind raced faster as I jumped out of bed and rushed into the dark living room before I stopped dead in my tracks, finally remembering where I was and what I was doing.

Max sat in front of the window with the blanket pulled away

from it only enough to peek out of. Drax was passed out on the couch, and Colt and Finn were nowhere to be found, so I assumed they occupied the other bed. Outside the apartment, the night still lay thick over the town like a blanket. I guessed I'd only slept for an hour or two before the panic wake up set in.

"It's probably the stress," Max said quietly. He sat perched in an old kitchen chair that he'd dragged into the room. "Happens to me all the time."

"What does the son of the most powerful man in the country have to be stressed about?" I scoffed.

"You'd be surprised."

"Oh no, not another crappy father situation, is it? Because we already have three of those issues going on." I nodded my head toward Drax as he lay peacefully on the couch.

"No," Max shook his head. "Quite the opposite actually." He fidgeted with his hands nervously as I pulled up a chair beside him. I could see the complexity in his eyes. Maybe his story wasn't as black and white as I'd thought. Maybe it wasn't as straight forward.

"I had a pretty good dad too." I smiled at the flood of memories that came back at the mention of his name.

"I bet he was great. You have to be to raise a daughter that grew up to change the entire country."

I blushed at his praise. It was odd, because it was like my brain was just now catching up to everything that was happening. A little sleep goes a long way when it comes to recuperating your strength. It was like I was finally rested enough for my mind to play catch up. I really just did a live broadcast in front of the entire country, basically telling everyone to riot against the powers that controlled them.

My dad would have been proud.

"He actually died five years ago, protecting some people on the purge night." My eyes still teared up every time I thought about finding him in the alleyway. It was the single worst day of my life, and that included the day I got summoned for the trials and the day we found out my mom had cancer.

"I'm sorry to hear that." Max reached out and laid his hand on mine. It was warm, and his eyes were sincere.

Slowly but surely, he was winning back my trust, and my heart maybe? I couldn't tell yet.

"Tell me about your dad," I wiped a tear from my eyes and changed the subject. "Is he a good leader?"

Max thought for a second before nodding. "Yeah he is, he's just," he thought for a second, carefully considering what word to lay down next. "Privileged. Let's go with that. He believes that everyone should have equal rights and that humans and supernaturals should cohabitate peacefully, but he doesn't want to make waves. He's afraid to take risks; he's afraid to protest and speak up and advocate. He worked so hard to get elected, and he wouldn't dare tarnish that cookie cutter legacy of his."

I looked at Max, who sat in the middle of the Vampire Trials, one of the most controversial rituals on the planet. I recalled him in the middle of the chaos that was the NHRA headquarters and how he looked right at home. He even went as far as getting killed on national television just to send a message about a cause that he believed in. "Well then how on earth did he raise someone like you?"

Max smiled, but it wasn't any kind of smile that I'd seen on him before. It was full of happiness but also full of just as much pain. "That would be my mom. She was his polar opposite in almost every way. She was fierce, and she was radical, and she wasn't afraid to speak up when she thought something was unfair. They actually met at Harvard. My father was getting a degree in magical politics, and my mother was just there to protest the unfair admission denials of humans. Even as she held her sign and picketed, he couldn't resist her charm. When he tells it, he always says that when he saw her, it was like he was seeing the sun, the moon, and the stars all for the first time. She was beautiful; she was talented, and she was human."

The last part threw me for a loop. *So he wasn't lying when he said he was human. He just wasn't telling the whole truth.*

"She died last year in a car accident, and my father hasn't been right since. But if I'm being honest, neither have I." He clamped his hands together so tightly that they started to turn red.

I knew the pain of losing a parent all too well, so I felt for him. I wanted to say something encouraging, something that would make him feel better like *the first year's the hardest.* But I couldn't lie. The first year wasn't the hardest; every year was the hardest. Sometimes it seemed like you would get over it; maybe you'd recover, and things would start to feel like normal. The truth was, no matter how hard you tried, you would never get back to where you used to be.

The old normal was gone, and all you could do was move forward with your life the way that they would want you to. If you were lucky enough, maybe you'd find a way to establish a new normal. But I don't think anybody was ever the same after losing a parent.

Max looked up at me, and our eyes met. I could tell he was being real, and he was being vulnerable, but most importantly, he was being *honest.* And even through the pain he was feeling, his honesty was sexy.

His brown eyes melted the anger around my heart and left nothing but admiration in its place.

"When she died, I wanted to continue her legacy, you know? I didn't want to hide behind my supernatural privilege and pretend that everything was okay because it wasn't. It still isn't. I want to create the future that she dreamed for me." He gazed out the window longingly. He went somewhere, retreated into the recesses of his mind. It was a look I knew well because I'd seen it in my own reflection one too many times.

"I'm sure she's really proud of you," I smiled. "You're doing really good work keeping her legacy alive."

He smiled at the words. I looked at him, and I couldn't even begin to imagine the hurt and confusion that he must feel every day. Half supernatural, half human. Too human for the supernaturals and too supernatural for the humans. He was a walking contradiction wrapped up in a handsome body, and I was sure that it was something that got to him every second of every day. He was trying to figure out where he belonged, what his place was in the world, and that was something I could sympathize with.

He squeezed my hand, and a rush ran through me.

"Was that your magic?" I asked as my hand tingled.

"What? You can feel it?" He looked confused.

I nodded. "It feels, electric. Like a static shock maybe, or my hand fell asleep. Is that not supposed to happen?"

"I don't know. I've never heard of a human being able to feel magic before, but anything is possible." I noticed he sunk his teeth into his bottom lip every time he was deep in thought, and I could tell by the look on his face that he was in deep.

The more I got to know him, the more I realized that I bonded with him. Shared trauma had a way of doing that to people, but this felt like something more. It felt deeper, just like the bond I felt with the guys. I hated to be an *everything happens for a reason* person, but I was glad that the tragedy of the trials brought something worthwhile into my life. It taught me that the heart wasn't constrained by society's views on love. Love grows and shapes itself in ways that we could never imagine, and in my case, it grew big enough to hold the hearts of four people. I made up my mind then and there that I didn't want to choose, and I didn't have to.

I grabbed Max's hand and pulled him across the living room.

"Where are we going?" he asked as I pulled him into the small room and closed the door behind him.

"To feel some more of that magic," I said under my breath.

The air inside the room was electric. It hung like particles on the breeze. Every time I took in a breath, it consumed my lungs and made my body tingle. All it did was make me want more of it, and more of Max.

I pulled him in, and our lips pressed together. My eyes opened wide at the rush of energy that flowed through his mouth and into mine. It felt like I was a bottle, and I was being filled up by his essence. It was electrifying and exciting all at once. Max didn't seem to mind at all as he slipped off his pants. He was more than ready, and I was more than willing. I didn't want it; I needed it. Something was pulling us together, and I wanted more than anything to feel him pulsating inside me. If his lips felt this electric, I wondered how electrifying his dick was going to feel.

Max pulled away and laid kisses down my neck, leaving little tingling pools of energy behind in place of his lips. It was hair raising, and it was toe curling.

I couldn't take anymore teasing. I didn't want any more foreplay. All I wanted was him, as deep inside me as he could get.

I used my strength to topple him onto the bed and assumed my place on top. I stripped down to nothing, letting the cool air rush over me before I made my way below his waistline and took him in my mouth. He was so big, I almost couldn't fit it all the way in, but I forced it inside.

I felt the same tingle of magic in the back of my throat, and it traveled between my legs. It was better than any vibrator I'd ever used. I sucked him off, and just when he was at the edge, I pulled him out of my mouth.

"No, not there," I moaned before I climbed on top and slid him inside of me. The tingles erupted into a wave of magical pleasure, and we both climaxed at the same time.

I threw my body onto his chest and rested my head beside his as we both panted for air.

"You mean to tell me this whole time I could have been having sex with witches? Nobody told me it felt like that!"

Max laughed. "Trust me, it usually doesn't." He moved a strand of hair from my face and caressed my cheek lightly. "There's something special about you, Scarlett Johnson. And mark my words, I'm going to find out what it is."

CHAPTER 24

The safe haven I felt laying on Max's chest was perfect. He was right; there was something special about him too. Something distant and familiar that lurked just beneath the surface of his skin. I couldn't quite point it out, but he felt like an old soul. Someone that I used to know in a life, long before the one I had. I didn't know much about witches, and I was learning that I didn't know much about vampires either. But what I did know was that I wanted to. I was sick of the generations of hatred and misinformation. I wanted to know the truth and figure out my feelings toward supernaturals myself.

We got dressed and quickly made our way back to the lookout post. Nothing had changed, but I wasn't about to wait until something did for us to jump into action.

"We should wake the others. If we move now, maybe we'll have a better shot at making it all the way into the city before sunrise."

Max nodded and went to wake Colt and Finn. Drax was already awake. He sat quietly on the couch trying to shake the haze of sleep that hung over him heavily.

"Are you guys sure you want to do this? The city is probably on fire, and if it isn't, it's about to burst into flames," I cautioned. "If you guys want to cut your losses and back out now, you can. You're already out of the city. It would be easy for you to disappear. Maybe start a life off somewhere in another country and never have to worry about getting killed for being near me ever again," I rambled, realizing my own insecurities may have added a few words here and there.

I looked up at each one of them, and I knew any of them would have walked through fire for me. They would die for me. They were all in. We started it together, and the looks on their faces told me that they were prepared to end it together too.

"All right, let's go before-" My words were cut short by the phase siren sounding.

Phase three. I wondered which phase it would be and prayed that fire didn't start raining down from the heavens. Fire was the last thing we needed that close to making it out of the games and into the city.

The winds outside picked up at an alarming rate.

"That's our cue to go," I said, but the guys were already scrambling into action. They were ready to head out the door before I was, and I was left trailing behind them down the narrow staircase.

I peered out of the barber shop window to see the wind violently whipping debris in every direction.

"I don't think they know where we are," Finn said quietly. "If they did, they wouldn't even mess around using the magic to sweep the whole city; they'd annihilate this little building the first chance they got."

He was right. I could hardly imagine the governors giving me a fighting chance, especially not after I basically brought the entire world to their front door. They would off me the first chance they got, nothing poetic about it. To the world I was brave, maybe even a martyr. But to them I was collateral damage. I was a threat to everything they held dear and every ounce of fictional power that they held in their hands. They wouldn't play games like this if they didn't have to.

We could use that to our advantage.

"Then now is the best time for us to move. We can't sit in here and wait for the tornado to come through and rip the entire city to shreds."

I yanked at the doorknob to try to pull the door open, but the pressure from the blowing winds fought it too much. It was too strong for me to fight against myself.

"Allow me, my lady." Max faked a curtsy before he held his hands up in front of the door. His hands vibrated and glowed a mystical shade of yellow before the door flung itself open like it was as light as a feather.

I raised a brow at him, impressed. Maybe there were some perks to sleeping with a hot witch.

"We have to go, now." I stepped out onto the sidewalk and had to try my hardest to anchor all of my weight into my steps. The wind was so strong that all it would take was a single slip up to let it send you toppling into the street. It felt like it was sucking all the air from my lungs; every breath was labored. It took a lot of work.

"This way!" I yelled, but my voice was swallowed by the rush of cool wind that swept through every street, so I motioned for them to follow. The subway entrance was just around the corner one street away, but it felt like it might as well have been worlds away by the effort it took to take a single step.

I thought of my mom. I couldn't give up. I had to finish this. I had to live to see her one last time. I didn't care if I dropped dead on the doorstep the second after she opened the door. I had to look her in her tired eyes one last time. She didn't raise a quitter. I wanted her to see that.

I forced one foot in front of the other, and right before I reached the other side of the street, a gun went off. I barely heard it over the rumble, but I saw the spray of bullets pelt the wall beside me. The wind was so strong that it skewed the trajectory of the bullets, and I'd never been more thankful for it.

I strained to turn and saw the shooter in the upper window of the building next to the barber shop. So close to where we were sheltered.

My heart raced. There was no way I could reach my weapon, and even if I did, I didn't have the shelter of the building to hide it from the gusts. The wind would have grabbed it and carried it away.

I stared in horror and watched as he was about to pull the trigger again.

Suddenly, the roof of the building was ripped off and consumed by a huge tornado as it swept through. It engulfed the building and devoured every part of it, the shooter included.

All it did was prove to me that in the trials, everyone was collateral damage. They didn't care about the people that they'd bribed to work against me. Their lives were almost as meaningless in the games as they were outside of them in the Governors' eyes. If they had to kill every person in the trials just to kill me too, they would have done it in a heartbeat. No questions asked.

"We have to go!" I screamed. The roaring tornado was approaching fast, but I could finally see the subway entrance. I tried not to think about the few hundred feet that stood between me and my own premature death. All I focused on was putting one foot in front of the other. Nothing else mattered to me. I finally wrapped my fingers around the metal railing that framed either side of the cement staircase that led deep into the ground. My heart thudded violently in my chest, and I clung to it as tightly as I could while the guys made their way to me. Finn made it in first, then Colt followed by

Max. Drax was the last one left. He was so tall and skinny that the wind threatened to whip him to the ground if he let it.

Come on Drax. Just a little further.

The suspense was almost too much to handle. If the trials took another person I cared about, I didn't give a shit. I was going to rip through the city like a wild dog and kill everyone in my path.

Drax grabbed my hand, but the tornado was so close now that it lifted his feet from the ground. I was the only thing that tethered him to the earth anymore, and even my feet were slipping. I felt Finn's warm arms wrap around my waist and squeeze me tight.

"I got you," he said softly.

Colt grabbed onto Finn, and finally, Max used his magic to pull us all in down the stairs.

The tornado charged toward the entrance and ripped it to shreds as we rushed down deeper into the subway system. Behind us was the deafening crack of cement smashing against the ground, and the tunnel went dark.

I pulled a flashlight from our supplies, and it flickered on, illuminating the entrance that was now a pile of rubble, packed tightly together.

"Well, at least we don't have to worry about that anymore," Max shrugged. He pulled out some extra flashlights and passed them out. Drax flung himself down on a bench to catch his breath, and Colt leaned up against the cold wall trying to catch his breath.

"Hey, can I talk to you for a second?" Finn asked. His eyes flitted to Max, and back to me. "Alone," he added.

It wasn't a suggestion.

"Yeah, sure," I muttered. I quickly scanned the long tunnel for a place we could have some privacy. My eyes landed on a small unisex bathroom and pulled him in its direction. I yanked open the door and cautiously pointed my flashlight inside. The last thing we needed was for another contender to get the jump on us, in the bathroom of all places.

Finn closed the door behind us and slid its lock into place.

It was the small kind that only had one stall in it, and a single sink. There was barely enough room for both of us to fit inside it at the same time, so I had to stand incredibly close. Our bodies nearly brushed up against one another.

"You wanted to talk?" I stammered, trying to ignore every instinct I had to rip his clothes off. What was it about almost dying that made me want to jump his bones? The adrenaline? The rush of knowing that I could die at any moment?

"Yeah," Finn's voice was low, and his eyes were determined, but I could tell being alone with me in such a small space was doing something for his instincts too. "Are you sure we can trust Maximus?"

He asked the question that had been plaguing me since we'd met him. But after the night before and everything he'd told me, I knew my answer.

"I'm positive."

Finn nodded. "You better be. Because I'm not about to take another bullet for you." I couldn't tell if he was joking or not; he had a habit of sounding angry all the time.

"I didn't even ask you to take the first one for me," I protested.

"You didn't have to." Finn brought his hand up to my face. "Sure, I hated you at first, but after I got a chance to see how bad ass you are, I'd die for you. For sure."

I laughed. "At least someone thinks I'm bad ass. It's like my brain can't decide if I am or not. Sometimes I'm just so angry at the fucking injustice that I feel no fear. But other times I feel so much fear that I feel no anger. There's never an in between. Does that make me bad ass?"

"It makes you human." Finn's face was only a few inches from mine. "And until I saw it on you, I didn't know how attractive it was."

Before my brain could grasp what was happening, his lips were against mine, and his body pressed against me. He grabbed me by my hips and set me on the counter before devouring my lips with his. I didn't remember when my suit came off, but it lay in a pile on the floor. Finn dug his fingernails into my back, and my back arched at the sharpness of his touch. I let out a small moan that he drowned in a kiss. His lips were delicious, but even more delicious was the sight of him ravenously ripping his clothes off. His eyes were full of lust, and his dick was overflowing with it. I sunk my teeth into my bottom lip at the sight of it standing at attention, waiting for me.

Finn didn't play any games. There was no time for foreplay; we both felt like we needed one another more than we needed anything. He thrust himself deep inside of me. It was rough; it was raw, and

I loved every second of it. The sex was like Finn, raw, steamy, and extra rough around the edges. I loved being dominated. I loved the look in his eye as he wrapped his fingers around my throat before pulling me in for a kiss. And I loved the way he pulled out and commanded me to turn around and bend over the countertop before thrusting himself back inside. He fucked me harder than I'd ever been fucked, and I didn't even know that I was into that sort of thing until it was balls deep inside of me.

"Fuck, Finn," I moaned. I didn't care if anyone else heard. There was something about Finn that pulled out the most seductive parts of me. I would gladly assume the role of a slut for him. I'd let him fuck me wherever he wanted, whenever he wanted to do it.

We both climaxed, and Finn looked at me with a devilish smirk on his face.

"When we make it out of this, we're doing that again. All night."

"Screw that, we're doing it all day too," I smirked. "But we have to make it out first."

CHAPTER 25

W e made our way back out of the bathroom, and surprisingly, none of the guys even batted an eye. They were all pretty focused on the fact that they'd almost died, and no doubt, were trying to make sure that it didn't happen again.

"We need to keep moving. Who knows what other tricks they have up their magical sleeves?" I picked up the supplies pack.

"We know fire is the last phase. And I'd hate to run into it down here, so we better move fast." Colt stood, ready to go.

I lead the way with my flashlight, and Max walked beside me. We moved quickly but being underground made me feel a little safer. At least we knew that the tornado couldn't get to us, or whatever other tactics they planned on using during the third phase.

Max and I walked up ahead, and the guys walked a little slower behind.

"So, what's it like?" I asked. "Living outside these walls? In the White house no less." The curiosity finally got to me, and I asked the question that'd been on my mind. I imagined all the freedom he probably had. All the restaurants he could go to, movies maybe. He could probably walk outside at night without being hounded by vampires cackling like hyenas.

"Believe it or not, it was lonely," Max sighed. "There's always some scandal being pushed in the media about my dad, or someone trying to extort or blackmail. When everyone knows who you are, it's hard to know who to trust. I was to the point where I couldn't tell the real people from the fake people anymore. I didn't know who wanted me for my spotlight, who wanted me for my money, or who wanted me just for me."

"That does sound lonely." My heart ached for him. I knew what it felt like to be surrounded by people but still feel the ache of loneliness deep inside your chest.

"It was, until I met you," he smiled at me. "Scarlett Johnson, the first person I'd met in years who didn't know who I was, and quite frankly didn't give a damn either."

I laughed. It felt good to laugh, even in light of the trials.

"If we get out of this thing, I'm going to take you on a date. A real, true, proper date. I honestly don't care if the three musketeers come with either."

I smiled.

"That would be nice." For a split second, I had hope. It actually felt like everything was going to be okay.

But it only lasted for that split second before my eyes caught on to a light far off down the tunnel.

"Hey, I see light!" I yelled to the guys behind us. "I think we're getting to the end of the tunnel!" I was relieved because every inch of my body hurt. I didn't know how much longer I could push on for. It matched up to the wall too. By my calculations, we were almost past the barrier and should have been making our way out of the tunnel.

My stomach lurched when I realized that the light was inching its way closer to us.

"It's a light at the end of the tunnel, but not the one we wanted," Max whispered.

The faint thrum of a siren sounded off far behind us, and it was clear what the light was. The final phase: fire.

We were trapped. Stuck between a rock and a hard place didn't even begin to describe the shit that we were in. I watched as the fireball sped down the tunnel and headed straight for us, and I had to accept the fact that there wasn't anything we could do about it. I couldn't spare them the pain that was about to come, and there was no way that they could spare me.

I looked up at Max with fear in my eyes and slipped my hand into his.

"It was really nice meeting you," I half smiled with tears in my eyes. Drax, Finn, and Colt joined our side. I looked at each one of them. "It was nice meeting all of you."

Tears streamed down my face, not because I was sad but because I was so angry at the defeat. Angry at the way I'd go out. So close to my freedom yet so far away.

Max looked at me. His eyes contemplated something. "Promise me about that date?" he asked.

"What? In the afterlife? Sure." I had no idea where he was going with his question.

"Everybody grab hands," he yelled.

Finn took mine, Colt took his, and Drax pulled in behind.

"It better be a damn good date." Max smirked, and we made our way toward the fire ball, slowly at first, but we picked up speed. The closer we got, the hotter the tunnel got. I felt like my skin was going to melt off.

"Whatever you do, don't let go!" he yelled. His hand glowed in mine, and my hand glowed in Finn's. It was a magical chain reaction that went all the way down to Drax. My hand tingled in Max's.

"Here we go!"

I squeezed my eyes shut just as the fireball washed over us. It was hot. Insanely hot. But suddenly it wasn't. I opened my eyes, confused, and turned to see the fireball traveling behind us. Max stopped in his tracks and panted.

A smile spread across my face. "You bastard, you did it!" I leaped forward and kissed him. He kissed me back before collapsing to the ground.

"Oh my god? Are you okay?" I panicked.

"A group spell like that is just a lot of energy," his voice was quiet and hoarse. "I'm fine. We have to keep going; we're almost there."

He was right. We needed to move fast, before they realized that we were still alive and sent another wave through.

Colt and Finn hoisted him up and helped him walk. With the fire out of the way, I could actually make out the faint light of the actual exit. I was right; we were past the tunnel. And if my calculations were correct, we would end up in the middle of Times Square. A bubble of hope rose up inside of me. Every step I took, I was one step closer to my mother, one second closer to seeing her again.

"Do you guys hear that?" The sound of people shouting was getting louder and louder as we made our way to the exit. It looked like the old entrance had been sealed off with steel panels. Small rays of light flowed in through the cracks.

"I'll go up and see if there are any handles or anything," Finn said. He closed his eyes and disappeared for a few seconds before he reappeared with his eyes wide.

"There are no handles, but you guys got to get up there. It's crazy."

"Can you teleport us one at a time?" I asked.

"I wish, but even vamp powers have their limits," Finn sighed.

"Let me do it," Max's voice was faint. "I have enough magic left in me to blast them open."

"You're so weak already," I protested.

"And if they find us down here like sitting ducks with enough time to send a second wave of fire, we're all dead. Let me do it." He sure was a stubborn witch, I'd give him that.

He pulled himself to his feet and pushed his hands up against the smooth metal. It took a few seconds for his magic to kick in, but when it did, the steel slates blew off and sailed into the sky. There was a loud crash as they crashed into one of the jumbo televisions and cracked it.

Finn caught him just as he collapsed, and it was a group effort to pull him from the cavern.

My mouth hung open when I stuck my head out of the entrance and witnessed the pure chaos that had erupted in Times Square. It was like a riot, as a horde of people rushed around. People clashed with human control officers, bodies lay in the streets. Cans of tear gas flew all around. I pulled myself from the entrance and stood in the middle of it all. I was engulfed in chaos, and for once, I didn't mind it a bit.

Someone noticed us emerging from the pit and screamed "It's her!" Over the chaos.

Even the human control officers stopped and stared at the five us emerging.

The first few seconds were tense. I had no idea who these people were, or what side of the fight they were on until a slow clap erupted into an uproar of applause.

All the jumbotrons switched to the same feed, the winner announcement. I read the words, and my eyes filled with tears.

"Scarlett Johnson, winner of The Vampire Trials."

I knew it wasn't over, far from it. But it felt damn good not to be part of the sick mindfuck that was the trials.

The happiness I felt turned to disgust as quick as it emerged when the screen changed and showed a live feed of the three governors. They sat at a desk, with their hands folded menacingly.

"Great job, Scarlett. Triad three must be very proud of you," the Governor of triad three said. Out of the corner of my eye, I saw Drax flinch just at the sound of his voice. "You know who else is proud of you? Your mother."

You bastard. You wouldn't dare.

"You know what? I think she has something she wants to say to you."

My stomach dropped to the floor as the camera turned to my mother. She had black circles underneath her eyes. I could tell she hadn't been getting her medicine. She looked weak and frail, even more so than usual.

"Go ahead, tell her to do the right thing and turn herself in," the governor urged off camera.

Tears were already streaming down my face. I couldn't handle seeing her like that. I couldn't imagine what hell they put her through because of me. But when she looked into the camera, I noticed something in her eyes that wasn't there before. There was a blaze of passion behind them.

"Scarlett, honey," her voice was almost a whisper. I was on pins and needles for her next words. The slightest smirk crossed her lips. "Do what your father would want. Burn this city to the ground."

ABOUT THE AUTHOR

Storm Song is a reverse harem fantasy author who writes characters who are just as much of a hot mess as she is. Not only do they learn to embrace the darkest parts of themselves, they're empowered to realize that no girl should have to choose between three supernatural hotties trying to crawl into her bed- Why not have them all?

Facebook.com/authorstormsong

Instagram.com/authorstormsong

storm song

Printed in Great Britain
by Amazon

56489776R00129